NIOMIE ROLAND

Laying His Claim

Anderson Sisters: Book 3

First edition

ISBN: 978-1-990122-00-2

This book was professionally typeset on Reedsy.
Find out more at reedsy.com

For my husband...

Contents

Chapter 1

"**A** couple hundred steps, and you're all done. Just five more minutes," Anna urged. "You're doing great."

"I can't!" Jalissa protested. She was exhausted and her whole body felt sore. She hated the hospital therapy room; to her it was nothing more than a torture chamber she was obliged to visit every day, to walk, push, pull, stretch, and roll. She felt like a puppy being trained.

"You can," Anna insisted. She placed a supporting hand at Jalissa's back. Jalissa was sure it was partly to encourage her and partly to keep her steady on the treadmill.

Jalissa wondered if Anna pushed all of her clients this hard. After all, it had only been two weeks since Jalissa had woken up from a coma and 18 months is a long time to be lying in a bed, insensible to the world. The doctors and therapists had all assured Jalissa that she was young and strong. They were confident that with the right therapy and care, she'd bounce back. Especially, they'd enthused, since she seemed to have such a loving group of friends who looked out for her; visiting often, sitting by her bedside, reading to her, even telling jokes, despite not knowing whether she could hear them or not. Jalissa chose to believe them.

"I *can*," Jalissa repeated, both to herself and her therapist. She ground her teeth in determination and gripped the handlebars, placing one foot in front of the other with deep concentration.

"*Ça y est,*" Anna encouraged. When she woke up from the coma, she was surprised to learn that she was also bilingual. French and English. Most people who lived in the Province of Quebec were. "That's it. You're doing great."

Sweat poured down Jalissa's forehead, stinging as it rolled into her eyes, but she stubbornly refused to wipe it away. Nothing was going to distract her from her goal. She wanted to walk with more grace and a bit of pep, rather than her current hesitant, almost painful movements that made her seem like the people in the geriatric ward. If every step was agony, then so be it. She'd work until her feet bled if she had to.

The treadmill wound slowly down to a stop and Anna clicked it off. "You did great, Jalissa," she said, and gave the younger woman a brief hug.

"Floor exercises now," Jalissa panted.

"Don't you want to wait a few minutes? Catch your breath?"

"No. Now." She dragged one of the padded floor mats away from the wall, smoothed it out, and lay on her back. The T-shirt and sweatpants she wore hung off of her body, hiding her thin arms and legs that were the result of being on a tube feeding for—she couldn't believe it—*a year and a half!*

The thought of it made her dizzy. No, wait, it made her angry. Mad as hell! Who wouldn't be after waking up to discover you have no idea who you are? As she began her routine, she studiously avoided her reflection in the bank of wall-to-wall mirrors in the therapy room. Why would she want to look into the face of a stranger? All she could see was a too-thin woman with huge brown eyes, warm brown skin, and natural hair that was carefully braided and drawn back from her face. Looking at herself evoked a vague feeling of familiarity, as if the woman in the reflection was a nodding acquaintance. She was someone who always arrived at the coffee shop at the same time she did every day on the way to work, so that over time they got into the habit of smiling and saying, "Good morning."

But what did she know about that woman on the inside? Who was Jalissa? Was she fun at parties? Was she kind? What did she like to read? *Did* she like to read? What about her family?

Jalissa stared up at the ceiling, divorcing herself from her own recalcitrant body as Anna moved her legs from position to position. She had no family; at least, that's what Kaiya had told her. That beautiful, serene, concerned woman who came to her hospital room every day, to hold her hand and chat. The woman who, the nurses said, had visited several times a week since her accident, to comb her hair, do her nails, and carefully apply a dab of lipstick to her lips.

Her *friend*, Kaiya, had told her. Her best friend since they were kids.

One evening, in the throes of a frightening dream, she had cried out for her mama. And that was when her new - old - friend had sadly informed her that Jalissa's parents were dead. No details, except for the fact that they had both passed before she'd turned eighteen. She'd been too dazed and exhausted to find out more, but she understood that she was alone in the world now, except for her friends.

"That's it, Jalissa. We're done for the day," Anna announced, stretching out her hand to help her up. Jalissa ignored it, rolling over onto her hands and knees before rising awkwardly. She was done hanging onto others just to stand or walk.

"I can make it back on my own," she said.

Anna beamed, "Wonderful."

* * *

"Knock, knock." Kaiya mimed knocking on the door jamb as she entered, making Jalissa laugh. If anyone could enter without knocking, it was Kaiya, who had been her rock during that awful, lost time.

Jalissa was sure there was something familiar about the fuchsia and turquoise design on the small bag Kaiya was swinging from one hand. It triggered a feeling of excitement and pleasure inside her, even though she couldn't connect the dots between the bag and her reaction.

Kaiya's quick, observant eyes were on her face and she broke out into a grin. "You know what these are, don't you!"

"Not exactly," Jalissa hedged, "But I feel... I'm certain it's something good."

Kaiya plopped herself down on the edge of the bed and bumped Jalissa with her hips. "Move over, woman!"

3

Jalissa slid over a bit, giving her ample room, unable to take her eyes off the bag.

"It's not something *good*; it's something *awesome!*" Kaiya plunged her hands in and brought out two clear boxes. Inside of them, Jalissa could see heavenly golden mounds of profiteroles, capped in chocolate and topped with cream.

She held out her hands like an eager child. "Give!"

"These are from your favorite patisserie," Kaiya explained, handing over a plastic fork.

Jalissa wasted no time. In seconds, her mouth was full of cool, fresh cream and magical dark chocolate. "I'm not going to argue with you there!"

When they were done feasting, they put aside the empty containers with satisfied groans. Then Jalissa was serious again. "Okay, cough it up."

"Cough up the profiteroles? Ewww!" Kaiya said in mock horror.

"No," Jalissa responded patiently. "Cough up whatever it is you want to tell me."

Kaiya shook her head in resignation. "And I thought you didn't remember me."

"I don't need to, girl. You're as transparent as glass."

Kaiya brushed some invisible crumbs off her stylish dress and asked hesitantly, "How are things going with you and Justin?"

Jalissa paused, not knowing how to answer. How were things with the grey eyed, dark-haired, tall stranger who everyone said was her fiancé? The one who came to visit bearing small gifts, brushed her cheek with his thick warm lips, and told her about his day for about an hour before disappearing again? What could she possibly say?

She barely remembered him and she sure as hell didn't remember getting engaged to him, but that's what he, and all the other semi-strangers who visited, had told her. There was Kaiya's husband, Tyler, and her sister, Kalilah, with her husband, Finn—who also happened to be Justin's half-brother. Lord, what a mess!

"Okay, I guess," Jalissa murmured.

Kaiya took her hand. "Girl, I know when you two were together, you used to

4

insist that it was all just for fun, but it's clear just by looking at his face that he cares for you. I could just punch you when I think that you got engaged without telling me, though."

When Jalissa didn't answer, Kaiya dropped her playful demeanor and looked her deep in the eyes. "Give him a chance, Jalissa. All he wants is for you to be part of his family, especially—" she stopped abruptly and withdrew.

There it is again, Jalissa thought, *that reticence. That feeling that there's something going on in the background. Something they're not telling me.* She felt a wave of intense frustration at being kept in the dark about her own life. "Especially what?" she demanded. "I deserve to know!"

Kaiya chewed on her cheek, not responding.

There was a real knock on the door and in walked Dr. Chiang, the consultant who had been supervising her care. He was accompanied by one of the nurses. "Mademoiselle Thomas, how are we today?"

"*We* are not in a good mood," Jalissa griped.

He came to stand by her bed. "Why not? You've been progressing admirably!"

Jalissa threw a dark look at Kaiya. "Maybe. But that's on the outside. Just because I can brush my own teeth and find my way to the toilet doesn't mean I'm whole again. I'm sick and tired of feeling like my entire head is nothing but a huge empty space. Full of... *nothing!*" she spat out.

He looked sympathetic, and explained, as he had before, "After your accident we detected no head or brain injury. Your psychiatrist and I are almost positive your memories will return. Unfortunately, there's never a definite timeframe with memory loss. But I assure you, my dear, that everything is still inside of you. All of your memories, your personality, your likes and dislikes, your relationships. You just need to give it some time. With therapy and patience, they'll come back to you."

Jalissa looked away from all the helpful, sympathetic faces. She wanted to believe what the doctor said, but...

The doctor threw a glance at Kaiya that Jalissa couldn't quite interpret. "As I have explained to you, Madame Anderson, the process must be gradual. You need to bear this in mind. It is not advisable that my patient receives too much information too quickly."

As Kaiya nodded her understanding, Jalissa looked from the doctor to her friend. What was that about? Information overload concerning *what*?

Dr. Chiang went on cheerfully, "Anyway, I have wonderful news for you. I've consulted with your other specialists and we have all agreed that you can go home in the morning."

"Home?" echoed Jalissa, stunned. "Tomorrow?"

The doctor was still smiling benignly, oblivious to her consternation. He checked her charts, made a few notes, *cluck-clucked* with the nurse, and then they bustled back out together.

Jalissa leaned back into her pillows, poleaxed.

"That's great," Kaiya enthused. "You get to go home!"

"But do I even... have a home?"

Kaiya considered this. "You used to have an apartment, but when the lease was up, I packed all your things and put them into storage. But don't let that worry you. You didn't think I'd let you go off to be all alone, did you? Of course, you're coming home with me."

"But Tyler..."

"Tyler won't mind," she admitted, "it's for the best. We're here for you."

The idea of going home to Kaiya's rather than being stuck on her own, to find a new place to live and learn to be human all over again without any help, brought a feeling of relief. There were still so many things she still couldn't cope with yet. Having a pillar of strength to lean on would be... A thought suddenly occurred to her. "Kaiya?"

"Yeah, Hon?"

"I'll come home with you, on one condition."

"Name it."

"That you don't tell Justin where I am."

Kaiya's brows lifted. "Why not?"

She was at a loss to explain. "I don't know. I just..."

"But he's your—"

"Fiancé. I know. It's just..." Jalissa grabbed her friend's forearm in desperation. "Promise me, Kaiya. Please. Just let me have some time on

6

my own to process..." she indicated her body with a wave of her hand, "all this."

Kaiya pondered, but not for long. "It's a deal, Babe. But just so you know, it won't take him long to figure out where you are. And when he does... all I'll say is when it comes to you and... Well, Justin always gets what he wants."

"What do you mean by that?"

"Well, as you know, I am your power of attorney."

Jalissa cut her off. "Was I yours as well?" She wanted to know how close they were before her accident.

"You were until your accident and since I was pregnant, and you were in a coma, I made Ty my POA."

"Understandable. Go on."

"During your coma there were decisions to be made—medically—and Justin and I disagreed on many things, but in the end I just gave in and did what he thought was best. Everything he fought for was in your best interest," Kaiya finished.

Jalissa pondered this. What else had been in her 'best interest', which Kaiya hadn't been happy with?

* * *

"That's it, Sebastian," Justin said softly to his son as he rolled the oversized Mickey Mouse beach ball across the lush carpet to the baby. Seb had just about mastered the art of sitting up on his own, something which never ceased to thrill Justin. The boy was seated just a few feet from his father, wearing nothing but a pale blue romper - Mickey Mouse again - a smear of applesauce, and a happy grin.

Seb lunged for the ball and tipped over like one of those inflatable bopper toys, bumping the carpet and springing back. It was all Justin could do not to rush over, grab him up and check for bruises.

Kids fall over, he reminded himself. And then they got up again, resilient as ever. Seb had managed to claim the ball as his own and was now enthusiastically sucking on it. This time, Justin intervened. "Oh no, you don't. Applesauce is for eating, balls are for playing, okay?"

Seb looked into his father's eyes adoringly and chortled as if he'd uttered the most hilarious thing.

Justin grabbed the ball and rolled it again, after which the two of them spent another happy fifteen minutes wrestling on the carpet, despite the fact that Justin's, now wrinkled, suit was a bespoke Brioni piece that had set him back almost six-grand. Who'd have thought a man like him would have gotten spit-up on his favorite jacket and just laughed it off?

When they were both exhausted, he lifted his son into his arms and walked over to the bench seat in front of the French windows that looked over his expansive estate. The gently rolling slopes of green were well manicured and, just under the window, he had placed several bird feeders so that he and Seb could sit and watch the little birdies. Though, if he were honest, the squirrels also claimed it as an all-you-can-eat buffet.

"See that, Seb?" he whispered into the child's ear. "That's yours. All of it."

* * *

"What a pretty picture!"

The deep voice penetrated Justin's light doze. He startled awake to find Seb snoozing in his arms where they were still curled up on the comfortable bench in the playroom. His brother, Finn, was standing over them, arms folded, looking amused as hell.

"What's so funny?" Justin griped, shifting Seb so the arm that had gone to sleep would finally have some blood circulating again.

"Nothing," Finn answered, still smirking. "Except for the fact that, even though it's been nearly a year, I still can't get over the sight of you looking all domesticated, rocking a baby to sleep. Who'd have thought it?"

"Oh, shut up," Justin responded with brotherly humor. "At least I've only got one. You're the one with three kids, Mr. Super-Sperm."

Finn took his ribbing gracefully and pulled up a chair. He cocked his head to one side, taking in the scene but saying nothing.

"Did you come all the way over here just to get all hormonal on me?" Justin

8

asked.

"Nope. I brought over some documents for you to sign. Regarding the Le Grenade land deal. I left them on the desk in your home office."

Justin nodded. "Okay." He waited. "And...?"

"And... I was just wondering how you felt about Jalissa being released. What're you going to do then?"

Jalissa. Just the sound of her name echoing in his mind reminded him of his own cowardice. Because he *was* a coward, cringing from the very thought of the consequences he knew he'd face from the moment Jalissa woke up from her coma.

The last year and a half had been hell for him. It pained him seeing her like that; stretched out on a bed, surrounded by machines, not moving, not speaking. Not even aware that he was in the room. It had been a nightmare.

There were those in the family who'd disagreed with him about decisions he'd made while she was in the hospital—but they didn't know everything. They didn't know what he knew about that awful night, a year and a half ago, when the two of them had torn into each other with cruel, angry words, saying ugly, hurtful things.

After an evening spent in a heated argument, Jalissa had let him know she was done with him. The relationship that had started as just a bit of fun was over and she wanted nothing to do with him. Then she'd roared off into the night on her souped-up Kawasaki, and away from him.

The next time he would see her would be in a hospital bed, bandaged from top to toe as she fought for her life.

They'd all been mystified by her accident. The police had said there'd been no skid marks at the scene of the crash, no other vehicle involved. Just a seriously injured Jalissa and a wrecked motorbike. The only person who suspected that the crash might have been Jalissa's attempt, in the heat of her rage, to harm herself, was Justin.

But he knew one thing; he wanted Jalissa to come home with him. He wanted her to meet his son, who had become the light of his world. If he could convince her to spend time with them both, maybe he'd be able to win her over. And, if he was lucky, she might fall in love with him -with *them*—before her memory came back.

Seb shifted in his arms, opened his eyes, and began to wail like an air-raid siren. Justin smiled indulgently. "Probably hungry."

"Considering the amount of applesauce all over his romper—and you—I guess he would be," Finn said with a smile. "Cause there's probably very little *inside* him."

Summoned by the wailing, the nanny, Lorena, came rushing in, holding out her arms. She was a pretty girl in her early twenties, with a smile that always seemed to get wider whenever Justin stepped into the room. Grateful, Justin handed him over with a few brief instructions about what she should feed him for supper. When she stepped from the room with the baby in her arms, Justin got to his feet to discover that Finn was smirking at him.

"What?" Justin demanded.

"She likes you, you know."

He frowned, puzzled. "Who?"

"Your nanny," Finn responded with an even wider grin.

"Bullshit," Justin retorted. He smoothed down his suit as best he could and began looking for his shoes. "*Tu parles de conneries.*"

Finn didn't bother to argue. "Where are you headed?"

"Hospital," he said simply.

Chapter 2

J ustin hated hospitals; the sickly smell of industrial disinfectant, and the pall of disease, suffering and death that always hung around them. He struggled to keep the sense of unease under control. This was the hospital that had managed to care for Jalissa throughout those long months of suffering and managed to bring her back to them. That was good enough for him.

As he rounded the corner in the hallway and approached Jalissa's room, the door opened and out walked Kaiya and her elder sister, Kalilah. They seemed excited, as if something was up, but the moment they saw him they stopped in their tracks. Justin couldn't help but notice that Kalilah hastily clicked the door to Jalissa's room shut and shifted her body to obscure it.

Immediately, he stiffened. "Good evening, ladies," he said mildly. Kalilah was his sister-in-law, and Kaiya was Jalissa's best friend. It was no use stirring up old antagonisms. Even though he and Kaiya had clashed over and over during the past year and a half concerning Jalissa's medical care, he couldn't deny that both women had Jalissa's best interest at heart.

"Hey," Kalilah said.

Kaiya nodded somberly. "Justin."

There was an awkward moment of silence until Kaiya broke it "How's Sebastian?"

It was a question that always brought a rush of warmth to him. "He's doing fine; sitting up, crawling around. Doing really well."

Kaiya smiled at this. "That's great." She looked as if she wanted to say something else. Justin waited on edge. "Jalissa's doing so much better," she told him. "She asked us to take her braids out, so she can work on brushing her hair herself. To strengthen her fine motor skills."

"That's a good idea." The two women were still standing with their backs to the door, facing him, almost as if they thought it was up to them to grant him entry. He was having none of it. "If you don't mind," he said calmly, "I'd like to see Jalissa."

Kaiya got that stubborn look in her eye that he had come to both admire and hate. "That depends."

He was incredulous. She was setting *conditions?* About his access to his fiancée? "On what?"

"On what you plan to tell her. She's making such good progress. It would be a disservice to... you know, do or say anything that would set her back. Remember, the doctor was very clear that her return to full memory should be gradual."

Justin cut in with frustrated impatience. He was well aware of the constraints involved in Jalissa's recovery, and even though his very soul chafed at it, he was willing to comply for her sake. "Do you think I'd ever do anything to hurt her? Even though, Kaiya, you of all people should know how secrets can get out of hand. The kind of pain they can cause."

At this, Kaiya's expression softened. "I know. I understand. I'm just trying to protect her—"

"*I'm* trying to protect her, too. It's the devil's dilemma. On the one hand, she needs to be prepared. She needs to be primed to accept the fact that... certain things happened while she was in the coma. On the other..." He stopped himself there, feeling his frustration rising and his temper with it. "Now step aside and let me in, ladies. She's my fiancée, goddammit!"

"So you've said," Kaiya snapped.

Justin wondered if the guilt showed on his face. "What?"

"She doesn't even remember getting engaged to you."

"She doesn't remember *anything!*" He realized he was shouting, and that was confirmed by the dirty looks two passing nurses threw his way. He blew out a hard breath and went on, "Kaiya. Kalilah. You've been pillars for Jalissa and I'm grateful for that. I know you two have known her way longer than I

12

have. But she's my fiancée, and I'd like to speak to her."

Kaiya and Kalilah exchanged glances, then nodded and stepped aside. "Be careful, Justin."

He ignored them, offended by the mere idea that he'd ever willingly cause Jalissa any hurt, and brushed past them into the room.

* * *

Justin walked in to find Jalissa sitting on the edge of the bed, her natural hair splayed around her face and shoulders in a poofy cloud. She gave it a spritz of detangler and began brushing.

He found himself fighting the urge to reach out and wind her thick tresses around his fingers. She was wearing a satin dressing gown that reached only to her mid-thigh. Far from the frumpy hospital gowns adopted by many long-term hospital residents, this one was black with bright splashes of red roses. Kaiya had done some excellent shopping on her friend's behalf.

One sleeve had slid off her shoulder, leaving it bare. He desperately longed to place a kiss on that expanse of smooth, bronze skin, but instead he said in admiration, "Like dandelion fluff on a summer's day."

She spun around, as if she hadn't heard him enter. "Hey," she said, smiling awkwardly.

He came to stand beside her, reaching out to tug on a lock of her hair. He remembered how it used to feel to wind handfuls of her hair around his wrists when they made love. How Jalissa used to urge him to tug on it with increasing roughness. The memory made him tauten, and he struggled to keep an even tone.

"You're doing a great job exercising your hands, working on your coordination. I know it must be a challenge."

She set the brush down and confessed, "Harder than walking, to be honest."

"The finer skills take longer to come back."

"I guess they do."

Jalissa picked absently at strands of hair in the brush, avoiding his eyes, and that pained him. He wished there were a way to take that anxiety away. He remembered how the old Jalissa, brazen and bold, used to parade around his bedroom without a stitch on, taunting him with the sheer perfection of her round bottom; the way her long legs scissored past each other as she walked. She was a woman who knew how powerful her attractiveness was and never ceased to use it to bring him to his knees.

And now, she barely trusted him.

If she didn't, how would he get her to agree to come home with him, where she belonged? *Spit it out*, he told himself, *it's the only way.* "When you're finally discharged, I want you to come home with me."

She resumed brushing her hair, and he sat beside her, taking in her profile, admiring the determination with which she persevered, in all things, large and small. But she didn't even try to answer.

"At least think about it," he urged. This time, he did touch her, his broad hand taking hold of her by the shoulder and turning her to face him.

At his touch, she inhaled sharply, then let her breath out in a gust. She set the brush down in her lap. "That's a very kind offer..."

"It's not about kindness, Jalissa. It's about *us*..."

"But it feels like I'd be going home with a stranger."

"First off, I'm not a stranger. I'm the man you love; the man you were going to marry." *Believe it*, he urged her silently.

Her brows lifted slightly at this.

He went on, "And second, even when I was a stranger," he countered. "You knew exactly how to handle me."

She gave him a look of surprise. "Did I?"

"You sure did. I remember being so mesmerized by you. You were fierce and loyal with your friends, especially Kaiya. And you were sexy and forthright with me. You never played games, never left me guessing. You knew exactly what you wanted."

Jalissa looked down at her hands, lying limply in her lap. "Not so fierce now," she sighed.

He tugged at the lock of hair again, then let it fall back into place at her jawline. "Maybe not now, but soon you'll be you again. Full of the old vinegar and spit. But in the meantime, let *me* be strong for *you.*"

That was enough for one day, he thought. If he pushed any harder, he would only come up against more resistance. Reluctantly, he stood up, excused himself with a peck on her cheek, and exited.

* * *

Jalissa let her gaze roam around the large living room of Kaiya's gracious home, taking in every detail; the curtains, the paintings, the furniture. The few bags she had brought with her were stacked in the guest bedroom, waiting to be unpacked. As it turned out, they were largely unnecessary, as Kaiya and Kalilah had shopped up a storm, filling the closet and armoire with clothes, shoes, and toiletries.

"This all feels so... familiar," she murmured.

"It should be," Kaiya responded. "You've crashed here a few times before..."

"Before the accident."

Kaiya grimaced. "Yeah."

Unable to respond, Jalissa reached instead for Kaiya's baby son, TJ, and Kaiya willingly handed him over into her arms. The baby didn't mind one bit.

She buried her nose into his curls and inhaled deeply. "I love the way babies smell. They're so—"

There was the sound of the front door opening and then slamming shut. Almost instantly, Justin appeared, followed closely by Tyler, who gave his wife an apologetic look.

"Jalissa," Justin said as he burst into the living room. Then he stopped dead, mesmerized by the sight of TJ in her arms.

"It's okay," she soothed. "I'm not going to drop him. My hands are steady enough. Besides, he's so adorable. I love the way he feels in my arms."

Kaiya and Justin exchanged glances, then Kaiya said, "Justin, she just arrived. Don't you think she needs a little time to settle in?"

"I don't think she should be settling in here at all," he snapped. "She'd be much better off at home with me."

"I'm not too sure about that—"

"I don't care what you think. She's my fiancée and deciding what's in her best interest is up to me—"

That set Kaiya off like a cherry bomb. "She's my best friend! I've known her all her life, so I think—"

"Cut it out!" Jalissa said, so disturbed by the war raging around her that she felt a wave of weakness threaten to overcome her. Tyler immediately spotted it and swooped in to steal TJ from her arms.

In a flash, Justin was at her side, looping his arm around her. "Are you okay? Do you want to sit down?"

His touch felt so good, his arms so inviting. But she resisted, shaking her head. "You have no right to fight over me! I'm not an imbecile!"

"Exactly!" Kaiya announced. "She can make up her mind, and she chose to stay here!"

"That's because you and your sister convinced her that she shouldn't come with me!"

"There's a reason for that!"

Tyler held up his hand. "Please, the two of you, Jalissa's only just left the hospital..."

"And she can make up her on mind about where she wants to stay," Kaiya cut in. "Can't you, Jalissa?"

Before she could answer, Justin shot back, "Not if she doesn't know the whole story—"

"What whole story?" Jalissa demanded, looking from one to the other.

"See what you did!" Kaiya growled.

Again, Tyler stepped in. "Everyone, please. Give her some breathing room. We all care about Jalissa; let's not drag her into some kind of tug of war."

Everyone paused at the sound of authority in his voice. He was calm, unruffled. "Now, Kaiya, I understand where you're coming from—"

"See!" Kaiya yelled.

"But that doesn't mean that, as a man, I don't feel what Justin feels. If you were in this situation, I'd want you home with me. No question."

Jalissa turned to look at him, struck by the protective love he was showing for his wife. In response, Kaiya calmed down. It was clear that she was now siding with her husband, and that made Jalissa feel almost betrayed.

Jalissa felt herself sway as exhaustion attempted to claim her. "I need... I need to go lie down..."

"I've done everything I can to make sure you'll be comfortable at home," Justin said gently. He tightened his grasp on her, supporting her whether she liked it or not.

She shook her head. "No... thank you, but no. This is all so confusing. I hardly know what to think. But for now, I'm staying here. Just until I'm able to manage things on my own." She gave Justin a look. "In my *own* home—once I find something."

At this, Justin flinched, but his defeat was clear. "Whenever you're ready to come home, to our life, you know where to find me." With that, he strode out of the house.

Kaiya gave Jalissa a sympathetic look. "Come on, girl, let's put TJ down for a nap, and then you can do the same." She gathered the baby into her arms and Jalissa followed them wordlessly into the nursery.

"Thanks," Jalissa said.

"I'll always have your back, girl." Kaiya settled TJ down into one of a pair of matching cribs, where the baby fussed for a minute, and then settled down to sleep.

Jalissa looked around the nursery, puzzled. "Why two?"

"Two what?"

She pointed. "Why do you have two cribs?"

The shock on Kaiya's face was there one moment, and then it was gone. "Oh," she said nonchalantly. "You know, baby sleepovers."

"Baby sleepovers are a thing now?"

"Yup," Kaiya said. "Now let's get you to your bed."

Chapter 3

I f she could say one thing for Kaiya, Jalissa thought, she treated her houseguests in style. The guest bedroom was something out of a lifestyle magazine, and the bathroom... Well, it was like indulging yourself in a spa treatment.

She soaked long and luxuriously in the sunken marble bathtub, inhaling the lavender and rosemary of the foamy bath bomb, allowing the essential oils to soothe her, body and soul. The compact speaker on the bathroom counter surrounded her with music that she didn't quite remember, but which delighted her nonetheless.

Reluctantly, she stood, allowing the silky water to drip down her legs. She'd promised to join Kaiya in the kitchen as she prepared dinner. She looked down at herself, still marveling at this newly reawakened body of hers, amazed by the fact that she could walk on her own, run her own bath. Such seemingly trivial things, but things of which she was justifiably proud.

As she toweled off, she took extra time with the slightly faded scars on her arms and legs, souvenirs of her motorcycle accident, no doubt. There were just a few nicks and scrapes, but most of her skin was smooth, brown and unmarked, so she assumed that with time, the scars would fade. Except maybe for that weird one on her abdomen, which was neat and slightly curved, like a smile, as opposed to the others, which were scary and jagged. She'd asked her nurse about it when she'd first noticed it, back in the hospital, but had only been told that she'd had to have a minor surgery while in her coma. The nurse had said little more, and Jalissa hadn't thought the scar was that much of a biggie if the surgery was necessary to save her life.

Jalissa dressed quickly, slipping a pretty rose-colored dress over her head, even though the high hem felt a bit revealing. Kaiya had done lots of shopping, and she was grateful for it, but many of the outfits were surprisingly skimpy with lots of bare midriffs and low necklines. She promised herself that when she had the time, she'd get herself some stuff that was more suited to her taste.

As she entered the kitchen, she realized that Kaiya was already there, busy at a large wooden chopping block, neatly slicing carrots with a chef's knife. "Hiya," Kaiya welcomed her cheerily.

"Hey," Jalissa responded, feeling a bit awkward about staring around at everything. The tiled backsplash behind the brushed chrome stove and the array of kitchen gadgets seemed to be whispering to her. Everything about her second chance at life felt so new.

She listened as Kaiya chatted away, wishing she could help herself to a small glass of ruby-red merlot from the same bottle she was liberally pouring into her sauce, but being on her meds, it wasn't a good idea. Just juice, then. "It's quiet," she commented.

"Lili's upstairs, probably doing homework. TJ will sleep for a while yet." Kaiya turned to stir her pot, humming to herself.

Jalissa felt a surge of admiration, almost a kind of longing, at seeing Kaiya so happy, so content in her role as wife and mother. She blurted, "What's it like?"

"What's what like?"

"This," Jalissa waved her arms around, taking in the gorgeous home. "All of this. Being a wife, having a family, raising kids with a good man. You seem so happy!"

"I am happy," Kaiya agreed. "It's good to know that all that awful stuff is behind us."

"What awful stuff?" Jalissa queried with a frown.

Kaiya paused. "Oh, man, of course you wouldn't remember, even though you were so much a part of it!" She poured another generous dollop of merlot into her own glass, joking, "We're going to need this when I tell you my story!"

They sat at the kitchen island on high stools while the pots on the stove bubbled merrily away and the aroma of rosemary chicken wafted out of the oven. She listened in fascination as Kaiya told her tale. How she had gotten pregnant as a teenager and how her parents had sent her away to shield their precious family name from the wagging of gossipy tongues. Then, as Kaiya's story got darker, Jalissa felt a chill come over her.

"I'm so, so sorry you had to go through that!" Jalissa gasped.

Kaiya paused, resting her hand on Jalissa's shoulder. "You were my rock through it all. Always there for me when I was grieved for the child I'd lost. And then when Tyler turned up in my life again, with his little daughter in tow, you protected me like a pit bull. You knew how badly seeing him again would hurt me."

"What a nightmare! I don't remember any of it, of course, but I'm glad I was with you; supporting you." Jalissa shook her head. "To have a baby and not know it! Imagine that! What kind of monster would keep someone in the dark about that!"

Kaiya leaped up, grabbed her oven mittens, and hurried over to the stove. "I need to check on the chicken." She couldn't even look Jalissa in the eye.

"But didn't you just—"

She was interrupted by a ruckus at the main door; two male voices raised, and... a baby crying? As if drawn by an invisible thread, Jalissa got up and walked carefully and steadily out to the front door, closely followed by Kaiya.

Tyler was standing just inside the foyer, and in the doorway stood Justin... holding a little boy in his arms. The men's voices were low, but it was clear they were arguing.

"Remember what the doctor said. Now is not the time," Tyler was saying.

Justin countered irritably, "Oh no? So, when is the time? Huh? When is the perfect time for something like—"

Jalissa was stopped in her tracks by the tableau before her, of Justin holding a baby in his arms as if he was born for it. If anything, he looked even more handsome, even more perfect. It was true what they said: a good-looking man was one thing, but place a baby in his arms, and he became irresistible!

Kaiya stepped forward, arms outstretched, cooing, and Justin immediately handed the baby over as if they'd done this a million times before. She leaned in and sniffed the top of his head, inhaling his sweet scent. Jalissa had grown used to seeing Kaiya holding TJ in her arms. She was the picture of a good mother. It was surprising and puzzling to discover that her friend's maternal instincts extended to babies who weren't hers. And, strangely, the tableau caused a rush of warmth to Jalissa's heart, even though she hadn't been around that many babies since waking up from the coma.

There was something about this one; something that pierced her to her very soul. Like a voice calling to her through the mist. She realized she was smiling like an idiot, just as gaga over the tyke as everyone was. "He's gorgeous!" she enthused. "What a beautiful, perfect little baby! Whose is he?"

The silence following her unanswered question echoed through the house.

"Well?" Jalissa demanded. Everyone was staring at her, and she didn't like that one bit. She turned to Justin as he retrieved the little boy from Kaiya's arms, sure that she could see a resemblance between Justin and the child. Not just a superficial passing connection, but something real and undeniable. The baby had his same straight nose and facial structure. The only thing different about them was their skin tone and eye color. The baby's were dark brown. The baby's hair was dark brown and curly, Justin's was straight and black.

The baby Justin had been holding when he'd walked in was his flesh and blood. His son.

The possibility was dizzying. It would mean that all the while she'd lain unmoving in a hospital bed, he'd been out there, fooling around and getting some other woman pregnant. Who was she? And was she still in the picture?

Kaiya said gently, too gently, Jalissa thought, "Jalissa, I think you'd better sit down."

"I don't want to sit down," she shot back, hating the tremor in her voice. "I want someone to answer me!" Then she sucked her teeth in frustration. "No, you know what? You don't need to answer. It's as plain as the noses on *both* their faces!"

Tyler took command of the situation. "Let's *all* sit down." He began walking to the living room and everyone followed. Justin sat on the love seat and patted the cushion next to him, inviting Jalissa to sit there. Something inside her longed to be close to him, to be next to him, but she wasn't sure what her reaction would be if she didn't like what she was about to hear. Besides, being next to him would mean being next to the baby. Some strange woman's baby.

Instead, she chose a chair opposite and sat, arms wrapped around her chest, trying to make herself small. Tyler took an armchair and Kaiya perched on the armrest. They looked so much in sync that Jalissa felt a momentary pang of jealousy. At least Kaiya would always have a man in her corner, a man who loved her and would be willing to throw himself in front of her to protect her from pain. What did Jalissa have? Lies. That was all.

"Jalissa," Kaiya began, but Justin held up his hand to stop her.

"No," he said firmly. "This is my story to tell." He turned a little in his seat to face her. The child was alert, looking curiously from one person to the other. His handsome face was somber and intense. "This is my son, Sebastian."

She knew it! She did some quick math in her head. The child looked to be less than a year old, which meant... "So what you're saying is, while I was in a coma, you were busy screwing some other woman? What's her name?"

Justin looked stunned. "What? No!"

"Well, that's the only explanation..." she snorted.

"There's another explanation," Kaiya cut in gently, shifting the baby from one shoulder to the other.

Justin got up, crossed the floor, and knelt before her, taking her hand. In his, her hand felt small and vulnerable. There was something about him that always made her feel like that. "Sebastian is your baby, sweetheart."

Her mind simply couldn't process what he was saying. "What do you mean? How? What..."

"When you had your accident, you were around six weeks pregnant."

"No!" she gasped.

"Yes, it's true. You were pregnant and I am the father. The hospital took good care of you, and you managed to take him to full term."

She looked around wildly, seeking confirmation, and finding it in a slight nod from Kaiya.

"The second crib in TJ's nursery is Seb's. We babysit Seb a few times per month," explained Kaiya.

She tore her hand away from Justin's. She couldn't stand to touch him.

What had made her feel protected by his touch just moments before? Now, it felt as if contact with him burned.

The baby's eyes were fixed on hers, in that eerie way they sometimes had, with an expression that told you they were looking into your very soul. And what frightened her was that her soul heard his call and answered. It was like a blow to the heart, an intense overpowering emotion that she had never felt before.

She leaped out of her chair and backed away. "No! Take him away!"

"Jalissa!" Kaiya gasped, looking horrified.

Justin looked like she'd slapped him in the face.

"How could you keep this a secret?" she demanded.

"What was I to do? The doctors advised us to not tell you anything that could cause setbacks with your progress. We were waiting for the right time. Do you think I would do anything to hurt you? Did you think I would turn my back on you? On him?" He stepped toward her, closing the gap between them. This time his voice was gentle. "Look at him, honey. Look at how beautiful he is. He has your eyes."

She clapped her hands over her face, trying to turn away but unable to. "I can't."

"You *can*," Justin affirmed, his voice coaxing, soft.

Finally, she lowered her hands until her eyes were uncovered and looked at the confused toddler. Sebastian *was* beautiful, with dark eyes like hers and curly hair. Surely it wasn't possible to fall in love in an instant. Was it? She felt thunder in her chest as her heart constricted and then swelled, opening up like a blooming rose. She was acutely aware of all eyes on her.

This is the explanation, she thought, *of why I always sense an underlying connection with Justin, why I feel as if I'm being tugged toward him on an invisible thread whenever we are together. Our DNAs are connected.*

What now?

Justin saw his opening and took the chance. "Your son needs you. He's been waiting nine months for you to hold him in your arms and take care of him. I'm begging you, Jalissa, come home to him. I promise you, everything is there for you. You'll be safe and comfortable. But most of all, you'll have all the time you need to get to know our baby. Don't you want that?"

She needed to think; needed to talk this through. How would she know if she was making the right decision? "Could you guys leave me and Justin alone for a bit?" she asked.

Quietly, Kaiya and Tyler got up and placed the baby in Justin's arms before leaving the room. Once they were alone, Justin and Jalissa faced each other. For several long moments, all she could do was stare at the picture they made, father and son. The baby looked about to fall asleep and was nuzzling the space between Justin's shoulder and jaw. Then he lifted his long, silky eyelashes and looked at her. In that very instant, her decision was made.

"This is all true?" she asked, although she needed no confirmation.

"It is," he replied simply.

"Then... then I think I should come home—I mean, to your place—for a little while."

A smile lit up his handsome features. "I'm so happy to hear that. Do you want to go get your things?"

She shook her head. In her fatigue, her body was beginning to feel like a weighty load she had to carry around, something independent from herself. "No, not tonight. I'm exhausted."

He nodded, looking concerned. "It's okay, Babe. I understand. Tomorrow, then?"

"Tomorrow," she promised. And prayed she was doing the right thing.

Chapter 4

J alissa stared around herself in amazement. While she'd packed her belongings, Kaiya had informed her that Justin lived in *the* most affluent neighborhood in Montreal—Westmount. On the ride here, she began to understand the emphasis. All the houses were mansions. Most of the homes had more than two-car garages, and she saw glimpses of children playing in their backyard pools. She saw women in training bras and tights jogging with strollers. Justin's house was just as grand and beautiful as the ones they passed.

He followed her appreciative gaze as they toured the house, and said proudly, "You should have seen it when I bought it. This place needed so much work but, thanks to Tyler, we were able to fully and quickly renovate it."

Turning slowly, Jalissa thought to herself, *This house is perfect.* Its under-stated elegance felt so much like Justin, it was as if his spirit had infused the building. The home contained three floors and a four-car garage. On the first floor, right next to Justin's home office, was her son's playroom. Justin joked that many people commented on the fact that it looked like Toy R Us. A large eat-in kitchen, formal dining room, living area and powder room were also situated on the first floor. The second floor of the house had five bedrooms and four and a half baths. The third floor apparently was used as his gym. Although they didn't go down to the basement, Justin told her that the basement was fully renovated and used as a media room.

The walls were filled with what she assumed to be African art. The entire home had a modern feel. White walls and large floor to ceiling windows that allowed for plenty of summer's sunshine to seep through. Pictures of Seb at different months lined the walls, and she leaned closer to have a look. The large furniture, artwork and style of the house felt like it was all him. Although she couldn't know that for sure since she barely knew him. Having expected to be tense and anxious, she instead felt soothed by the colors and the fresh, free-flowing air. It was almost like a homecoming.

"There you are!" came a chirpy voice. A pretty, curvaceous young woman came hurrying in, arms outstretched toward Justin in a silent request for him to hand Sebastian over.

Before doing so, Justin made the introductions. "Jalissa, this is Seb's nanny, Lorena. Lorena, this is Sebastian's mom, Jalissa. She's back from the hospital."

The woman gave Jalissa little more than a curt nod, and then immediately, her eyes were on Justin and Seb again.

Rude, Jalissa thought.

The baby was half asleep, but as he was passed over, he fidgeted and became fussy.

"Oh, hush now, my dear, sweet boy," the woman cooed.

Jalissa felt a tiny prickle under her skin. *Whose* dear, sweet boy? She reached out to pat the fussy baby on the head, but the younger woman deftly skirted her with a quick, sharp look, swooping away possessively.

"Just change his diaper, please. Then bring him to us," Justin instructed.

The woman nodded, still throwing looks at Jalissa as she walked away.

Seems a bit possessive for just a nanny, Jalissa thought, but before she could say anything, Justin took her by the arm gently. "This way."

With one final glance at Lorena, who was disappearing down the hallway, still cooing at Sebastian, Jalissa allowed herself to be led farther into the house. They came to a large, well-lit room, which was filled with exercise equipment. Quickly, she spotted a treadmill, a stationary bike, two types of workout benches and some light weights. "What is this?" she gasped.

Justin held her in his somber gray gaze. "This is your therapy room. I had it set up for you as soon as you woke up. What's more, I've arranged for a physiotherapist to come in and work with you three times a week."

"*Oh my,*" she breathed in disbelief. "You did all this for me?"

"Of course." There it was again, that intense look that she couldn't tear her eyes from. "I'd do anything to make sure you're safe and happy. I want nothing more than for you to be fully recovered and mobile again."

Justin had done this for her. Jalissa was so grateful she wanted to hug him—but didn't dare. Then he was moving again.

They finally went upstairs and came into a beautiful bedroom with a queen-sized bed, a large armoire, and a dressing table on which several unopened packages of makeup and toiletries were arranged. She guessed that the door on the far end led to an en-suite bathroom. Justin had thought of everything. For a moment, she felt ashamed for having initially refused to come with him when he'd obviously spent so much time thinking things through.

There was a sound behind them and both spun around to see Lorena standing there with the baby in her arms. He was wearing a fresh new onesie and rubbing his sleepy eyes. "Thanks, Lorena," Justin said, taking his son from her.

The woman just stood there, as if waiting for something. Again, Jalissa felt that warning prickle at the back of the neck. Why did she get the impression that the nanny didn't like her?

"That will be all for now, Lorena."

A shadow crossed the woman's face before she spun about and walked off. By now, Jalissa's curiosity levels were boiling over, but Justin was striding off again. She followed him to the most gorgeous nursery she'd ever seen. She didn't want to think about how much all those fancy toys and decorations cost!

Jalissa stood just inside the doorway, mesmerized by the scene before her. Justin, this tall, masculine, gray-eyed man, could also be someone who rocked a little boy to sleep, crooning nursery rhymes into his hair, kissing the smooth little forehead, and then patting him on the back as one tiny thumb found its way into his mouth. The love filling the room was palpable.

Justin straightened and smiled. "Hungry?"

"Now that you mention it..." she smiled back.

Together, they walked to the kitchen, and Jalissa marveled that she instinctively knew where it was. It was as if the house were whispering to her. She watched as Justin quickly put together a light meal, complete with fresh salad and homemade vinaigrette. They then walked out to the patio which looked out onto the expansive lawn.

They sat at the table in comfortable silence, enjoying every morsel and appreciating each other's company. As the empty plates were pushed away, Jalissa had to ask, "How long have you had Lorena working for you?"

Justin thought for a second. "Since Seb was two months old. I'd taken some time off to be with him, but eventually I had to go back to work."

"And you're... happy with her?"

He quirked a brow. "She came from a reputable agency and she seems to love Seb. Why?"

"Nothing," she responded with a shake of her head. Reaching out, she put her hand on his arm and wondered when was the last time she'd touched him like that of her own volition. "Justin..." she paused to lick her lips. Just the feel of him against her fingertips tingled and her mouth suddenly felt dry. "I want you to know how much I appreciate all that you've done for me..."

He gifted her with that slow, lazy smile of his. "I know everything you've gone through has been a shock, especially finding out about Seb, but I want you to know I'm here for you. Both of us are."

* * *

Justin sent Lorena home earlier than usual. It had been a good day, and he was sure he and Jalissa would be able to handle the baby for the rest of the evening. Besides, he wanted to be alone with her. There were so many influences acting on her emotions, so much pulling and tugging, that he was grateful for the chance to bring her some peace.

They ordered in for dinner and he was glad to see Jalissa eat with gusto. During her time in the coma, she'd become so thin that he was determined to get the meat back on her bones by tempting her with all of her favorites. Her favorites were realized by bringing her multiple cuisines, desserts and snacks when she woke up from the coma and got sick of hospital food. Unsurprisingly, she still preferred gourmet meals over fast food. She was a chef before the accident.

The three of them ate dinner in the informal dining room. Seb was seated in his highchair with his own bowl of mashed potatoes and squash and, though his eyebrows ate most of it, he managed to get quite a bit into his mouth.

"He's not going to bed like that, is he?" Jalissa asked, half joking.

"Of course not. Let's give the old man a bath, shall we?"

She got to her feet eagerly and the three of them headed into the bathroom where Justin ran a tepid bath and laid out everything they would need: calming lavender soap, bath sponge, towel, baby powder, diaper and pajamas. As he stripped the baby off and set him gently into the water, Jalissa stepped forward. "May I?"

Justin tried not to show it, but inside he was elated. The Jalissa he knew would never have volunteered to bathe a baby. "You sure you know how?" he teased.

"I have no idea," she grinned. "You're gonna have to teach me."

They knelt side by side at the edge of the tub as he gave her soft instructions. "It's all about common sense, really," he said finally.

"You're assuming I've got that," she joked.

"You've got common sense in abundance," he said softly, looking into her eyes.

Once the baby was clean, leaving them both damp, they dried Seb and moved him to the changing station where Justin watched Jalissa sprinkle him liberally with baby powder. Then she tried to put his diaper on.

"The design goes in *front*," Justin pointed out.

"Oh, shut up," she quipped. When she got it on correctly, they helped Seb into his pajamas, and then—there really was a God—she took the boy into her arms and cuddled him. Justin was so afraid to ruin the sanctity of the moment that he said nothing. Just looking at them was enough proof that everything he had done to ensure Sebastian's welfare, every lie he'd told, was all worth it.

"Do we put him in his crib now?" Jalissa asked.

"Not yet. Our little guy needs a bottle before bed or else he'll never fall asleep. I'll go get it."

Justin hurried to the kitchen, grabbed a bottle, and hurried back, not wanting to miss a second of this bliss. By the time he'd returned, Jalissa was ensconced in the wooden rocking chair, holding the baby in the crook of one arm, and had an open Dr. Seuss book in the other hand; *Oh, the Places You'll Go!* Justin liked to think it was one of Seb's favorites.

Seb took the bottle gratefully, while Jalissa giggled in delight as the bubbles rose inside it, replacing the milk that was quickly going down into a very hungry tummy.

When the story was finished, they put the little sleepyhead down and stood side by side, watching him with admiration as his dark eyes closed.

He turned to Jalissa, and she was glowing. *How beautiful she looks*, he thought. *Motherhood looks good on her.*

Then she stifled a yawn, and he felt a pang of guilt. "You must be tired. I've kept you going too long."

"Don't be silly. I had a nap." Then she yawned again.

"And you're going to have another one." He walked Jalissa to her bedroom door, and for a moment, they stood there, wavering. Eventually, he pointed down the hallway. "I'm down there, at the end, if you ever need anything."

"Okay," she said simply.

"Goodnight, Jalissa."

"Night."

He waited until she shut the door before turning and heading to his room.

* * *

It had been a great day, Justin thought. Just the fact that she had agreed to come home with him had made it so. As he showered, he reflected on the image of Jalissa holding Seb in her arms. It had been so perfect.

He was filled with hope. Maybe his plan would work and she would fall so deeply in love with her son that when her memory finally returned, and she realized what had happened before she'd had the accident, it wouldn't matter.

Sliding naked between the sheets - he always slept in the nude - Justin tried to settle down for the night, but had a devil of a time doing so. All he could think about was Jalissa, just down the hall, in her own brand-new bed. He remembered that she, too, liked to sleep in the nude and wondered if she still had that habit, or if it was just one more element of her personality that had been swept away by her injuries.

He longed to touch her. For a few brief moments he entertained a fantasy of himself walking down the hallway to her room—still naked—and slipping into her bed. If he did, would she welcome him?

Stop that, he griped irritably to himself. She needs time, not just to recover from her injuries, but to adjust to the strange and life-changing circumstances she had woken up to. He promised himself he'd be patient.

Then the baby monitor next to his bed lit up like a Christmas tree, the LED lights glowing in response to Sebastian's wails. He wasn't a let-them-cry-it-out type of father; he believed that when your child wanted you, you went to him. Quickly, he tugged on a pair of sleep pants and walked briskly to the nursery, only to find Jalissa had beat him to it, even though her room had no monitor.

She was bent over Seb's crib, gently patting him on the tummy, and already the cries were slowing. She glanced at him and whispered, "Hi."

He enjoyed what he was seeing so much that he was momentarily unable to speak. Eventually he stepped closer and responded with a quiet, "Hey."

Seb snuffled and went quiet, drifting off to dreamland.

"Great," he said encouragingly, "but you need your rest, too. Go back to bed. I'll stay with him awhile; make sure he's sound asleep."

"I'm good," she said.

"No, really—"

"I said it's fine, Justin," she insisted with old-school-Jalissa firmness.

He knew better than to argue. Together, they stood over the crib, watching that small, beautiful human sleep.

Chapter 5

J alissa stood at the bay windows in Seb's nursery, looking dreamily out onto the expanse of lawn. With the neatly tended shrubbery and the quiet suburban roads just beyond the walls, she felt a tremendous sense of satisfaction and calm. It had been a good day. She'd slept in, waking to find that Justin had waited to have breakfast with her.

When he'd popped out on business for a few hours, he'd left Lorena to supervise Sebastian's care. The woman had literally locked herself and the baby in the nursery. Curious, and a little offended, Jalissa had pressed her ear against the door to hear Lorena's voice, reading from the same Dr. Seuss book as she had the night before.

Jalissa liked to think that she'd done a better job of reading aloud. She certainly was better at doing all the little voices!

Justin had returned with lunch and dismissed Lorena early. The nanny had looked none too happy about that. Now, as Seb crawled around at Jalissa's feet, she had the feeling that everything was going to be all right in her world... as soon as she got her memory back. She heard a sound behind her and didn't even bother to turn around. "I love your view, Justin."

He came to stand just inches behind her. Jalissa could feel the warmth emanating from his body, but resisted the urge to lean back against his chest.

"Would you like to see it up close?"

Jalissa twisted around to look into his face. "What?"

"Let's go for a walk."

"I don't know if I'm ready to handle the rough terrain," She whispered.

But, as always, Justin was encouraging. "You'll be fine. We'll stick to the beaten path. It will help bring strength back to your legs and put some color in your cheeks."

"Are you saying I have sallow cheeks?" she teased him.

"Not at all. But a breath of fresh air will make you glow."

The rolling expanse of land on Justin's property gave her a ripple of excitement. "Yes," she agreed enthusiastically. "Let's."

Shouldering Seb, he offered the other arm to Jalissa. She took it gratefully, only mildly embarrassed to admit that she still needed the physical support, but not looking forward to the prospect of pratfalling in front of him.

The freshness of the air hit her as soon as they entered the garden. She paused, closing her eyes and inhaling. "Lovely," she said dreamily. She opened her eyes to catch him staring at her.

"Yes, it is," he agreed emphatically.

Jalissa had the feeling he wasn't taking about the scent in the air.

They walked side by side, comfortably in step. Several times, he asked if she was okay, or if she needed a rest, but her pride wouldn't let her stop. "I'm just a poor old coma girl," she joked, "but I'm not an invalid."

"I'm glad," he said. "I'm glad you survived all you've been through. I'm glad you're okay."

Instead of answering, she lapsed into contemplative silence, mulling over his words.

Justin led the conversation, reminiscing about growing up in Ottawa with Finn and his twin sister, Violet. He talked about what it was like to have Finn as an older brother, and she was surprised to learn that Finn was their mom's biological child, but that Justin's father came into the picture when Finn was a few years old. But, a good man and a loving father, he'd adopted Finn immediately upon marrying their mother and made him his son.

Jalissa had the feeling that he was subtly trying to re-introduce himself to her, to recreate the memories of stories he surely had shared with her before. She was grateful to him for trying.

"My family has always been in the restaurant business," he said. "Most of them are in Ottawa, but we have a couple under management in a few other cities, including Montreal. We grew up in the business, the three of us. We learned all aspects of it from a very young age. Our dad insisted that we learn to do everything, including bussing the tables and working the grills."

"I guess that means you make a mean burger and fries," she joked.

"I honestly do," he smiled at her. "From scratch, too. Even our pretzel buns are homemade."

"And do you plan to go into the business full time? I mean, when your parents retire?"

A shadow passed over his face and for a moment she wondered if she'd put her foot in her mouth. "I guess I will, eventually, even though Dad intended to hand the business over to Finn..."

"Finn!" she said, surprised. "How come?"

He shrugged. "I guess because he's the eldest. But he's so deep into the business with his in-laws, that he's said he wants no part in it. So, it falls to me."

Jalissa wondered briefly how Justin felt, knowing that his father had offered something of such real and sentimental value to his half-brother, rather than to Justin, his biological child. But she knew better than to ask. It would do no good to pry where she was probably going to be unwelcome.

Instead, she decided to change the subject, to steer the conversation in a lighter direction. She turned to him, smiling. "Did you—" It must have been nothing more than a pebble, but in her weakened state, it was enough to turn her ankle. Jalissa felt nothingness underneath her and knew she was falling. Sky and grass spun into a blur—and then a strong arm held her fast.

"There you go," Justin said soothingly. He made sure she was steady on her feet, but even then, didn't release her. Instead, he pulled her closer. She could feel the solid expanse of his chest against hers and the warmth of his body, even through his light jacket.

She was locked in, unable to move, tormented by a single question that repeated itself in her head over and over: *What would it be like to kiss him?*

He seemed to be wondering the same thing as he lowered his head, so close that she could feel the light puff of air as his breath fanned her face.

Then came the now-familiar grunt that always preceded Sebastian's cry, and they were both treated to a high-decibel blast of sound that one could hardly believe could emanate from a package so tiny. They both turned to stare at him... and the spell was broken.

Justin sighed. "I think the little guy's hungry."

"I guess we should head back, then." She had to struggle to hide her disappointment.

Of course, Murphy's Law being what it is. A light sprinkle of rain sprang up as soon as they were within sight of the house. Justin placed one hand over Seb's head and pressed him closer to his chest in an effort to keep him dry. Instead of approaching from the front, where they had exited the house, he led her to the closest doorway; the garage. "Faster this way," he explained.

Laughing with excitement at the unexpected sprinkle, she stuck close to him, past the low-slung silver BMW he drove for fun and the safer and more sedate SUV he drove when Sebastian was with him.

Then she spotted something propped up against the wall, and immediately, she could identify it by brand. A Kawasaki motorbike, sprinkled with a fine layer of dust, but even so, it was clear that the paint job was firehouse red.

It was also clear that it was hers. *Her* bike. She stopped dead, wondering, *how do I know this is mine?*

Jalissa walked toward it as if in a trance, reaching out to touch it, stroking it as though petting a horse. She could sense its power. She'd ridden this? How had she found the courage?

"I had it fixed for you," Justin said. "It used to mean a lot to you."

The beautiful object didn't have a scratch on it. Judging from the extent of her own injuries, she could imagine the mess it had been in after the accident. "You fixed it... and kept it here for me?"

Justin was smiling now. "You practically treated it like a pet!"

She ran her hand along the tough leather of the seat, closing her eyes and trying desperately to form some kind of connection with it. Would it speak to her? Would it help her to remember... anything?

There was nothing but silence from the cold, dead machine. Because that's what it was, a machine, not a living thing. Certainly not a pet. She withdrew her hand in disappointment and backed away. "I appreciate the gesture, Justin," she choked out, "but I'll never ride this... this *thing* again!" She rushed into the house, leaving him and Seb to follow.

* * *

"Jalissa?" Justin called as he walked through the house. She had only been there a few days, but already he had fallen into the routine of seeking her out the moment he came home.

Lorena was in the kitchen, feeding Seb, and the interior of the house was quiet. He headed for the home gym where Julissa spent most of her time lately. He admired her for being so determined to heal and become stronger.

The door was open and, as he stepped inside, he was treated to a sight that stopped him in his tracks. Jalissa was doing bent-over rows, her back to him. Headphone wires leading to her ears let him know she couldn't hear him approach, so instead of announcing himself, he stood there and enjoyed the view.

She was wearing nothing but skin-hugging, cherry-red workout tights and a black sports bra that left her midriff, back and shoulders bare. A few days of good eating was beginning to show and her slight frame was already rounding out. *Starting*, he thought, *with her butt.* Which, as luck would have it, was pointing right at him, like a red flag before a bull.

He felt an erection rising, and it took a lot of self-talk to bring it into check. He remembered the feel of those smooth brown mounds of flesh against his bare thighs; Jalissa used to love it when he took her from behind, because it freed his hands to fondle her dark, hard nipples. She'd loved it when he grasped her hair and pulled it taut, groaning lascivious words into her ear about what he was going to do next, and how much she was going to enjoy it.

That little trip down memory lane had done nothing to alleviate his erection. It was at full mast. *Down boy,* he thought as he entered the room awkwardly. As she re-racked the weights, she noticed his approach. She grinned at him; face sweaty, the flush of exercise in her cheeks—reminding him of another circumstance when he used to see her flushed and sweaty, and now the pain in his groin was damn near unbearable.

"You okay?" she asked, frowning into his face with concern.

36

"Great," he managed. But a voice inside his head whispered, *No, not great. I won't be great until I take you on the floor, right here.* With much effort, he silenced it. She simply wasn't ready. All he could do was keep his desires under control until the time was right.

He realized she had asked him a question. "Sorry? What was that?"

She smiled. "I was wondering if you'd take me shopping."

"Sure. It'll be good for you to get out of the house. What do you need? Books? Are you bored?"

"Clothes."

His brows shot up in surprise. "Clothes? I thought Kaiya had practically brought you an entire trousseau."

"I'm not ungrateful, but," she looked down at her exposed, sweaty midriff with a rueful smile, "most of these are a bit... I dunno, revealing."

He chuckled. "Well, I'm not complaining, but I'd be happy to take you shopping."

She gave him a quick hug and then immediately stepped away. "I'll just go shower."

* * *

It was funny how little things could bring him pleasure, Justin thought as he followed Jalissa from boutique to boutique at the mall in downtown Montreal. Most men complained loudly about the trials of going shopping with women—and, truth be told, he used to be one of those men—but he was having *fun*. Go figure!

"Do you like this?" She held a pale blue dress up against herself, swaying slightly as she admired her reflection in the mirror. It was beautifully cut, with the skirt falling to the knee and a pretty, off-the-shoulder neckline that would show off her lovely, smooth throat without being too revealing.

"I do," he said sincerely.

Happily, she added it to the growing pile of outfits she wanted to try on. "Now," she announced, "let's go see if they fit!"

The salesgirl removed the hangers and handed Jalissa a small square of wood with the number of outfits she was taking in printed on it. As Justin moved to follow her in, the woman stopped him. "I'm sorry, Monsieur, but you aren't allowed back there."

He'd suspected as much, but Justin wasn't the kind of man who took no for an answer; he hadn't risen to the position of wealth and power that he had now by doing so. Negotiation was everything, he believed. Deftly, he removed a sizeable currency note from his billfold and slipped it to her in a smooth gesture. "She may need my help to zip up," he advised. The woman took one glance at the money in her hand and stepped aside to let him pass.

Win.

Jalissa chortled as she yanked the curtain to the dressing booth closed. "I guess money talks."

"Volumes," he agreed soberly. "Now, let's see how these look on you."

Jalissa treated him to a mini modeling show, and Justin enjoyed every second of it. When she tried the blue dress she had liked, she spun around, admiring her reflection. "I can't believe it; can you?"

"Believe what?" he asked.

"How different these things are from the kinds of clothes Kaiya bought for me. Half of them look like I'm heading clubbing, and the other half, well..."

"I am not complaining," he joked.

But her expression was sober. "I can't shake the notion that this look is new for me. I'm pretty sure Kaiya bought clothes for the friend she remembered. Am I so different now, that clothes like that just don't feel like me?"

"You're different, all right. But that doesn't mean to say there was anything wrong with the way you used to dress. You'll still have plenty of opportunity to embrace your glamorous side."

She seemed to accept his idea. "But for now, I'll stick with classically stylish."

"I like that idea." The proximity forced upon them by the small booth reminded him of how deeply aroused he'd been earlier, seeing her sweaty from a workout, and that desire was threatening to overcome him again. It felt as though with every passing moment, his need for her grew.

To his relief, she gathered up an armload of clothes and announced, "I'll take these."

He slipped out behind her, back into the shopping area, where the salesgirl was still waiting. She was gleeful from the tip Justin had slipped her and her eyes glowed even brighter when she mentally calculated the commission she'd make on Jalissa's armload of garments. Before Jalissa could even try to get her purse out, Justin was already handing over his credit card.

She threw him a surprised look. "Thank you, Justin."

"My pleasure." The emphasis was on *pleasure.*

It was too much for the salesclerk who giggled excitedly. "You two are so cute! Are you shopping for a vacation? Honeymoon?"

Jalissa politely told her no and hurried away, as if stung by the implication that she and Justin were a couple. As for him, he was highly amused. He decided to taunt her. "We do make a cute couple, don't we!"

"Oh, hush," she said, and picked up her pace.

As they headed through the store toward the exit, they both noticed a kiosk at the same time. It was half-hidden under a mountain of stuffed animals. "Ooh!" she said excitedly. "Let's get one for Seb!"

Justin smiled. "Seb already has a dozen teddy bears."

"But does he have a stuffed," she grabbed up a toy, "*iguana?*"

"No," he said gravely, regarding the odd-looking little beast indulgently. "He does not, in fact, have a stuffed iguana."

"Now he does," she announced.

The purchase was made, and they walked out to the parking lot, Jalissa cradling the big green toy, which she had decided to name Cucumber, and Justin carrying the shopping bags. He loaded the things into the trunk and then made sure she was settled in the passenger seat. When he was seated too, he made no effort to drive off. "Thanks," he said.

"For what?"

"For a lovely afternoon. For your company. For being so great with Seb."

"You've been great with him all this time," she reminded him.

"Maybe," he agreed, "but that's nothing compared to the care his mother can give him. And you have been awesome."

He wished he could say more, but he was overcome with emotion. She was

39

trying so hard, struggling against great odds, and he admired her so much for that. And then the admiration was swamped by a wave of desire, so he leaned forward and kissed her.

Her cry of surprise was stifled by the pressure of his lips. A moment of shocked resistance was replaced by a softening and opening, as her lips parted for him. He was thrown back into the past, reminded of the many times they'd kissed with hunger and passion. So many stolen moments at the start when they sneaked around behind everyone's back, while Kaiya, Ty, Kalilah and even his brother Finn were barely aware that something was going on between them.

He remembered how they'd acknowledged that instant, gut-wrenching attraction and gleefully abandoned themselves to what was supposed to be a fun fling. Back then, their kisses were wanton, outrageously so.

This kiss was nothing like that. There was the memory of their hunger, yes, but more importantly, there was the satisfaction of having this intimate contact he'd yearned for so long.

Jalissa made a tiny sound, and he lifted his head. Her eyes were wide, fixed on his face, enquiring.

Shame washed over him and Justin cursed inwardly. He'd promised to bide his time, to wait until she was strong enough to handle a moment as intimate as this, but he'd jumped the gun. "I'm sorry, Jalissa."

She hastened to reassure him, as if aware of his embarrassment. "It's okay—"

"No, it's not okay. I shouldn't have pressured you."

"It's fine." Her lips tugged up into a nervous smile.

"Okay," he conceded. Then he started the engine and put the car into gear. As they drove off, he noticed that she was holding Cucumber tightly in her arms and leaning away from him, against the door of the car.

Chapter 6

It was the perfect day for a pool party: blistering hot, with all the shrubs and flowers around Justin's estate dancing in the light breeze. It had been several days since that moment in the car, and still, Jalissa wasn't able to get over it. Justin's mouth had felt so perfect against hers, so familiar, but not quite. It bothered her deeply, knowing that she'd once been intimate with this arresting man. The fact that Sebastian existed was proof of that. But not being able to remember it disturbed her. *A kiss from a stranger who was not a stranger.* How did you wrap your head around that?

Over the past few days, the two of them had stepped around each other awkwardly, being super polite but avoiding each other's gaze. They were as careful and loving with Seb as before, but took it in turns rather than play with him together. Even when handing him over from one to the other, they made sure not to touch each other. Lorena seemed to have picked up on the vibe and looked gleeful, making a big show of being extra good with Seb whenever Jalissa needed a break or whenever Justin was around.

She was really beginning to have uneasy feelings about that woman.

"Here you go," Kaiya said, handing Jalissa a virgin cocktail and settling down into the lounge chair next to her friend. She held up her own glass, which held a frosty honeydew melon cooler. "*Santé*, ladies!"

Kalilah and Kaiya both raised their glasses and took a sip, then turned toward the large infinity pool, inlaid with aquamarine and silver tile work. The ladies might have been content to sit around enjoying the sunshine, but the men were having none of it. Justin, Ty and Finn were splashing around like grade-schoolers, trying to keep up with the actual children: Lili, Milania,

Maximillian, and Myles, while the babies, TJ and Seb, squealed in their fathers' arms.

It was a welcome-home party of sorts, Justin had explained, to celebrate the progress Jalissa had been making. For Jalissa, it was a great distraction from the awkwardness between herself and Justin.

"Careful, Jalissa. If you keep staring at the man so hard, you might accidentally set him on fire," Kalilah said.

Jalissa was startled out of her thoughts. "Huh?"

"You've been staring at Justin for the past, like, two hours," she said with a grin. "What's up with that?"

"Nothing," she insisted, but she could feel the flush rise in her face.

"Uh-huh," Kalilah said dryly.

Kaiya inched closer. "Something happened, didn't it!"

Jalissa looked away, and that was all the confirmation the other women needed. "Ooh!" Kaiya squealed, laughing. "Details!"

"No details," Jalissa responded irritably. "We just kissed, that's all."

Kalilah piped up. "Honey, if Justin Tremblay is anything like his brother, I'll bet there's no such thing as a 'that's all' kiss."

"Well..."

"Well?"

"It's just that everything's so weird between us now. We're both so antsy around each other."

"That's just the attraction talking, girl," Kalilah advised her.

Jalissa knew she was right. The attraction between her and Justin kept growing and growing, and pretty soon she was sure it would become so great that their coming together was inevitable. The idea thrilled her, excited her, and scared the heck out of her. His magnetism and presence were so great that she was afraid it would blow her away. So, she didn't answer. She *couldn't* answer.

Kaiya, bless her, came to Jalissa's rescue, changing the subject. "Seb's going to have his first birthday pretty soon. Are you excited?"

Jalissa had to admit she was, especially when she considered how weird it was that she hadn't been "present" at his birth! "I am. I don't even know how to celebrate! I mean, what do you do for a one-year-old's birthday party?"

"Knowing Justin, he's probably already got something grand in mind," Kaiya pointed out. "So, ask him."

"I will," she said, but she squirmed at the idea of having to say anything more to Justin than, "Good morning" or "Do you think Seb's hungry?"

"Don't worry. Judging from the looks he's been giving you all morning, I'm sure he's open to conversation."

It was as though Kaiya was reading her mind, best-friend style. Even with all the horseplay and the constant hopping in and out to get the kids some juice or a snack, Justin seemed to have plenty of time to check her out. It made her hot with pleasure, even though she didn't dare admit it to herself. And she, in turn, had been throwing sly glances his way. In his navy-blue board shorts, he was the epitome of fit, toned and tanned masculinity. Very easy on the eyes indeed.

"He's probably taken with that hot little swimsuit you've got on," Kaiya said. "I'd never have figured you for a one-piece, but it really shows off your curves. Is it new? Cause there's that silver bikini I bought you."

Jalissa didn't want to seem ungrateful, but the string bikini Kaiya had picked out for her had made her feel a bit, exposed.

Kaiya went blithely on. "And don't forget you have loads and clothes and other stuff from your old apartment in the storage unit I rented for you. You should check it out."

The idea of going through her own possessions as if they belonged to a stranger made Jalissa a bit nervous, but she knew it was time. Surely it would help her move toward recovery, maybe even jog her memory. "Thanks, I'll do that."

"I've got the keys in my bag. Remind me to give them to you before I leave, okay?" She got to her feet and waved her cocktail glass. "I think I'm going to have another. Who's joining me? I know you've got to have a virgin cocktail, Jalissa, because you're still on your meds, but what about a margarita, Kalilah?"

Her sister shook her head. "Nah. I think you'd better make mine a virgin too."

"No alcohol? On a beautiful day like this. Did you lose a bet?"

"Nope," Kalilah came back at her with a sly grin. She patted her tummy. "I guess you could say I won something…"

Her two friends gasped. "You're pregnant?" Kaiya squealed.

"Uh-huh." Kalilah was beaming with pride, and Jalissa felt a moment of jealousy. What did it feel like to be so much in love, and so excited to carry your husband's baby? What did it feel like to give birth?

Instead, she swallowed her hurt and gave her friend a hug. "Congrats."

Kaiya hugged her sister too. "I know Finn's a football fan, but I never expected him to try to build his own team!"

Beaming, Kalilah said, "we're making up for lost time."

* * *

The beach ball whacked Justin in the head and bounced harmlessly away. Apparently, he hadn't fully registered when his niece, Milania, had yelled out, "Uncle Justin, catch!" before executing her throw.

"I'll catch it next time, sweet pea," he promised as she swam away to retrieve it.

"That's what you get from being distracted by a beautiful woman," his brother said at his elbow.

"'Scuse me?"

"You've been staring at Jalissa all morning," Tyler informed him, standing on his other side. The three men leaned back against the wall of the swimming pool, water up to their chests, while the babies paddled within arm's reach, now secure in their little animal-shaped flotation devices.

He could have denied it, but it was true. The sight of Jalissa in that dazzling one-piece swimsuit was so alluring that he was glad he was submerged in water; it would help cool his desire. Since that kiss in the car, things had been uncomfortable between the two of them, and he'd give anything to lessen that tension.

"How's she doing lately?" his brother asked.

"Great," he said with admiration. "She'd getting stronger. She works out

44

on her own for two hours a day; her physiotherapist has helped a lot, too, but even she has said it's time for Jalissa to strike out on her own."

"And her memory?" Tyler asked delicately.

Justin shook his head. "Not much progress."

"That must be hard," Finn said.

"She's a trooper."

"She is, but I meant hard on *you*. Being in love with someone, being ready to marry someone, and then *bam*, they don't even remember you."

Justin couldn't stand the look of sympathy his brother was giving him, especially since it made him feel like a fraud. 'Love' was a loaded word, and as much as he liked, admired and desired Jalissa, he wasn't sure it applied to this situation anymore. As for their "engagement", well, he'd done what he'd had to do, given the circumstances.

His mind was dragged back to that terrible night; the night of the accident, when she'd revealed her pregnancy to him, and then said so many cruel things before storming out. *"I don't love you! I want nothing to do with you! I want no ties at all!"* He remembered the pain, the twist in his gut as he'd watched her go. That had been the Jalissa of the past. Did he love the Jalissa of the present?

Better to not say anything, he thought. "I'll go see if the kids are ready for their hot dogs," he said and walked to the shallow end of the pool.

Once the kids were fed, they begged, pleaded and badgered their way back into the water, and this time, the women joined them. Kalilah and Finn shared their news, and Justin felt a spark of joy. He clapped Finn on the back. "Way to go, brother. Making me an uncle again, huh!"

"I hope one day you'll return the favor," Finn responded, grinning proudly.

Immediately, Justin's gaze flew toward Jalissa. She was holding Sebastian in her arms, playing a splashing game, and the sight of them together drew him irresistibly to her side. "Hey," he said.

She smiled happily at him, "Hey."

He searched her face for signs of the version of Jalissa who had stormed out of his house screaming and yelling that night, but found none. What he saw was a mom who was enjoying a moment of sunshine and fun with her little boy. It warmed his heart.

"Throw the ball to Daddy, Sebastian," she urged. The baby batted ineffec-tually at the ball and went into peals of laughter.

They played with him for half an hour and to Justin, it was a perfect moment. The awkwardness was forgotten and, once again, Seb was the glue that bound them together. They were like a family.

"He's getting so big," she commented admiringly. "I can't believe he'll be one soon."

"We're going to have the party to end all parties," Justin promised.

"The girls said you'd say that! What are you planning? A house party? Kids' Zone?"

"We'll think of something," he assured her. For now, he was simply content for it to be just the three of them, together.

Chapter 7

Jalissa and Justin stood under the harsh lights of the storage unit and looked around at the neat piles of boxes. Kaiya, God bless her, had carefully packaged everything from Jalissa's apartment into separate identical boxes, and then labeled each one: Kitchen, Bedroom, Books, etc. Immediately recognizing her intent, Justin flicked open a Swiss Army knife and slit the tape that sealed each box.

She began slowly, starting with less personal items, like kitchen equipment and books. She was surprised to see how many kitchen gadgets she had, and while she didn't remember much about brand names in the culinary milieu, she wasn't so ignorant that she couldn't recognize quality when she saw it.

Had she really used all of these expensive items? What sort of food did she cook? Jalissa hesitated, glancing up at Justin. He nodded, encouraging her to go ahead.

She ran her fingers along the smooth brushed chrome gadgets, enjoying their understated sleekness. There were the usual items, like blenders, stand mixers, can openers and juicers, the kind you'd find in almost any kitchen. But there were also machines that spoke of a woman who enjoyed her time in the kitchen: hand-mills, pasta makers, bannetons and the like.

There was an exquisite set of knives that looked deadly sharp, and so perfectly made she could balance each of them on the tip of her index finger. She found a set of cast-iron pots that looked well-aged and used. She hefted a skillet and stared into it as if she expected to find answers to the mystery of who she was inside it.

"I guess Jalissa liked to cook," she murmured.

Justin came to stand behind her, placing his hands on her shoulders. "Yes, she did. Probably still does. Made a career out of it too."

She wasn't so sure about that. She replaced the skillet into its nest of packing peanuts, almost sorry it was so well insulated, because she'd have liked to hear it make a satisfying *thunk.*

Then came a box of music CDs, ranging from popular hip-hop to sexy, sultry R&B. *Bedroom music,* was the term that crossed her mind. Frantic, frenetic house music, alternative and trance, ribald dancehall... that told the tale of a woman who liked to party, and party hard.

She thought of how Justin's sound system back at the house was usually set to play smooth, sophisticated jazz, and modern instrumentals, and how soothing she found their vibe. Had she really been into those loud, crashing melodies?

With each box she opened, she felt as if the storage container had become a time machine, taking her back to a past she didn't remember, and forcing her to confront a woman she didn't know.

She glanced up at Justin, who was standing close, looking down at her as she knelt before the boxes. She wished she could read the expression on his face. Since that kiss, they'd been awkward with each other for several days, but things had calmed down after the pool party. They'd become more relaxed around each other, albeit not best buds. What was he thinking? Was he looking on at all the treasures she was extracting from the magic cave of her past and judging the person she had become or the person she used to be?

There were many boxes of clothes. She opened the one closest and began unfolding each item, holding them up before her like she was back in a store, shopping, wondering if they would fit, and, more importantly, if they would suit her.

No, they would not fit, Jalissa of the past had been much curvier, lavishly so, even. But those long months in a hospital bed had taken their toll, and she'd of course have lost some weight. True, Justin was on a campaign to put some meat back on her bones, and she'd been gaining enough weight to not look like someone who'd been confined to a hospital.

But worse, these flimsy scraps of fabric belonged to a stranger. There was no arguing with the labels; it seemed that she always bought the finest of the finest, but the low-cut blouses, micro-mini skirts, tight shorts and sheer fabrics left her feeling a tiny bit shocked.

As for the underwear... well! Teddies and thongs, push-up bras, *crotchless panties?* Really? She felt heat suffuse her face, a sense of embarrassment, a feeling as if she was invading another woman's privacy, going through her hostess' dresser drawers at a party.

She noticed Justin eying the lacy bra she was holding aloft. It was scarlet, studded with diamantes which she was sure couldn't possibly be comfortable, and had tiny bows on the shoulders which, when tugged, would allow the entire garment to be whisked away. She wondered if he'd ever seen her wearing it or whether he'd ever helped her *out* of it.

The flame in his eyes told her he had. Another red flush suffused her dark skin. "Did I really dress like this?" she asked him in wonder.

"You did, and you were beautiful in everything you wore. You cared a lot about your appearance and I loved that about you." He dropped to his haunches beside her. "The first time I met you, you were wearing a crystal-encrusted leather body-con, with a diamond-shaped neckline. You glowed. I couldn't take my eyes off you."

She searched his eyes to see if he was telling the truth, and when she realized he was, she looked away. He'd fallen for a Jalissa who wore waist-clinchers and gems. Would he—or anyone else—even look twice at a Jalissa who wouldn't even dream of wearing a skirt that barely covered her thighs?

In disgust, she dumped the bra back into the box, scooped up the other articles of clothing strewn around her, and shoved them into the box; trying to push them down so hard that she wouldn't be able to lay eyes on them. She realized she was panting, as if she'd been running.

"That's not me anymore," she declared vehemently. "Those aren't my clothes. They could never be."

"Who you are now is just fine. And your clothes are perfect," he assured her.

She wasn't sure she believed him.

Start digging again, she told herself. Maybe you will find the person you are looking for. She homed in on a box that was labeled Personal Items. Justin stood by her side as she pushed back the flaps, but didn't intervene. She was grateful for this; she was glad to have him there, but for this box especially, she felt that this was something she needed to do by herself.

One by one, she withdrew the items and examined each carefully before setting them down beside her. School reports; high school yearbook; immunization records. Even a little plastic box labeled Jalissa's baby teeth. This almost made her smile. Her mother had kept everything!

A small framed photo caught her eye: featuring a young, brown-skinned couple embracing each other and smiling at the camera. The man was tall and handsome, smart looking in a three-piece suit; the woman's wedding gown flowed behind her. They were standing in front of an elaborate five-tiered cake covered with white sugar roses.

In the man's eyes, in his smile, she saw her own.

"My parents," she gasped. It had to be.

"Yes," Justin said simply.

Kaiya had told her that they were dead, and had died while she was quite young, but inexplicably, she missed them. If her mother had been alive, would she have sat by Jalissa's bedside while she was in a coma, as Kaiya had?

There was a large manila envelope marked Mom and Dad in a handwriting Jalissa had come to recognize as her own. She shook out the contents. There were faded birth certificates, including her own, and a death certificate for her mother: cancer had been the cause of death.

Upon checking the date, she realized that she'd only been ten when her mother died. How had that affected her? Had it been heartbreaking for her? What had it been like, growing up without a mom? How had that helped her become the person she had been, whoever that was?

"Did I remember her?" she asked Justin.

"I think you did," he replied gently. "I think it was hard on you. You sometimes talked about how difficult it had been going through your teen years without a mom to guide you."

She nodded and reached into the envelope again. A heavily embossed letter fell out, with the logo of a large national insurance company printed on the envelope. Hesitantly, she opened it and unfolded the piece of paper within. "Dear Sir," it began. "We regret to inform you..."

She read through to the end, becoming more and more angry as she went. Her father, it seemed, had been very ill. From the date on the letter, she deduced that he'd been sick with whatever it was that had eventually killed him.

With cold, officious politeness, the letter informed him that his claim for future medical coverage had been denied due to...

"A preexisting condition?" Jalissa wondered out aloud.

"You told me he'd died when you were about eighteen."

"From what?"

He thought about it for a while. "I think you said it was organ failure."

"Organ failure?"

There was a sheaf of documents and invoices with dates covering the last few years of her father's life, and the amounts were staggering. She could only imagine the financial devastation he'd had to endure. But why?

Gently, Justin took the documents from her hands and replaced them in the envelope. "Why don't we look at happier things? Leave this for another time? When you're more able to work it through."

Her curiosity was overwhelming, but he was right. This was so hard, trying to decipher the secrets hidden in piles of old documents. She continued going through the box, finding knick-knacks and mementos. Carefully wrapped Limoges figurines belonging to her mother, her modest wedding ring and other jewelry.

She smiled wryly when she discovered that her mother had kept all her report cards; and laughed outright when she read the comments of her teachers, which said the same thing over and over: *Jalissa is a bright student who would do much better if she stopped playing around in class*, or, *Jalissa would go so far if she developed more respect for authority.*

"Kaiya told me I was a little hellion in school."

"And now you have proof!"

He was smiling as he looked at her, and in his deep gray eyes she saw amused admiration. She wished she could hug him—but that was a dangerous desire.

At the bottom of the box was a large black photo album. It weighed five pounds and took both hands to wriggle it free from the debris. It was expensive, leather-bound, and embossed in gold lettering were the words: Our Family.

She placed it flat on the floor of the storage container and knelt over it, almost afraid to open it.

Justin seemed to understand her hesitancy. "It's okay," he soothed. "I'm here for you."

Slowly, she turned the pages, taking in the round, smiling face of the little girl she had been but didn't recognize, and the man and woman who seemed so proud of her, so loving, but who were now strangers to her and her memory.

Her heart constricted. Having parents you couldn't even remember was as bad as not having parents at all. She was an orphan of the mind.

Feeling the breath catch in her chest, she returned to the album. Halfway in, the smiling woman in the photos began to grow thin, and later began to wear something on her head that was obviously a wig, as the color and texture was nothing like what it should be.

There were photos of Jalissa's 10th birthday party; a small affair, it seemed, with a much younger Jalissa standing at the table about to cut the cake with a woman in a wheelchair—a pale, jaundiced shadow of a woman.

Those were the last photos of her.

Jalissa choked down a sob, putting her hands to her lips to force her grief to stay inside. She felt Justin's arm around her shoulder. "We can stop now," he suggested. "There's always tomorrow."

"No." she was surprised at how mulish she was being, but the pull on her heart was irresistible. She kept on turning the pages. The photos that followed were of her and her dad, who had been a large, healthy-looking, barrel-chested man—until Jalissa was about fifteen or so. Then the process began again. Loss of weight, skin slowly growing pale, gray this time, and then, nothing. He was gone, too.

She let the photo album slip from her nerveless fingers, overwhelmed by grief. Why did it hurt so much? Who were these people that she should cry for them? And most importantly, who was she, the girl in the pictures who looked so happy?

When Justin took her into his arms, she went willingly. He slid his hand around to the back of her head and pressed her face against his broad chest. The muscular expanse was like a rock, but the arms that held her were gentle. She cried it out, for some reason not feeling embarrassed to show him how she felt at this moment. Her instincts told her that she was safe.

Jalissa wondered how many times she'd sunk into his arms like this. Had her past self often needed comforting like this? She suspected not. Had there ever been a moment when she was in a crisis, when he'd had to dry her tears? Or was she the kind of woman who never let them see you sweat, never let them see you cry?

And if that were the case, then the vague sense of familiarity, that déjà vu she was feeling would be for something else. If he hadn't held her with compassion, he'd held her with desire, with lust.

As her sobs abated, she began to wonder; what had it felt like to be in his bed, in his arms? What had making love to Justin been like? Was it long, slow and gentle, or fast, demanding, greedy? And how had she liked it? Did she enjoy being under him, on top of him, side-by-side, freeing her arms to reach out and caress? Did he bring her to orgasm fast, over and over, or did he torment her, make her beg?

She lifted her head to look at him and to her surprise realized he was looking down at her intently. It was impossible to understand the emotion hovering behind his eyes. Immediately, she withdrew, feeling overheated and awkward.

What was he seeing when he looked at her? What was he feeling? Was he missing Old Jalissa? Did he wish she was that woman again, the woman with the crystal-encrusted dress and the red bra? The woman he'd intended to marry, and who he'd insisted, had said yes to his proposal?

Of course, he missed her. Who wouldn't? Old Jalissa was confident to the point of being brash, bold and daring in her tastes. She reveled in her own sexuality. That woman had no problem laying herself bare—literally—and reveling in the unabashed looks of appreciation from men.

But she was no longer that woman. She had no idea who that woman even was! Whoever Justin was expecting her to be, she knew now she'd never be that person again.

She wrenched out of his arms and stood, putting a few paces between herself and him. He stood, too, looking confused. "Jalissa, what's wrong?"

"Not her," she muttered through gritted teeth.

"What?" He hadn't heard her.

"I. Am. Not. That. Woman!" she clarified, jabbing her fingers in the direction of the unfortunate box of skimpy clothes. "I'm not her!"

He misunderstood. "You will be, eventually," he soothed. "I promise. It will come with time."

"No!" Her voice rose, echoing off the metal ceiling of the storage container. "I never want to be her again!"

Frustrated, she began grabbing up her mementos, the family albums, her parents' correspondence, her legal documents, and shoving them into the Personal box. She huffed as she lifted it off the floor, causing Justin to grab it from her before she keeled over.

"I've got this," he said.

She was so upset she couldn't even thank him. She flicked a lock of hair behind her ear and scanned the room, making sure there was nothing important that she was leaving behind. "I'll put this in the car and then we'll come back for more," he said.

"No."

"No?" he was puzzled.

"I don't want this. Any of this. These," she waved her arm angrily in the direction of the boxes, "these things aren't mine. None of them!"

He was obviously trying to be patient. "Well," he asked cautiously, as if afraid to set her off again, "what do you want me to do with them?"

"I don't care, Justin! Can't you understand that? Burn them; sell them; donate them. Whatever. I just don't ever want to see them again."

He had the good sense not to argue. Instead, he hitched up the box and stepped through the roll-up door, and stood aside for her to step out. He locked it and mutely handed her the key. She took it with a nod, a bit ashamed of her outburst but not ready to let it go. Instead, she began leading him out to the parking lot. "Seb's waiting at home," was all she said.

54

Chapter 8

I t took just two more weeks of hard work in the home gym for Jalissa's physiotherapist to inform her proudly that she no longer needed to continue her thrice-weekly sessions. "I'll only need to check in with you just once a month, from now on," she said. "Isn't that great?"

"Wonderful."

The two women parted company and, after Jalissa saw her off at the door, she turned and headed up the hallway to her room, mopping up the sheen of sweat from her forehead. She'd worked so hard, and even though it had been agonizing, exhausting, even boring, she was miles away from the place she'd started, when she could barely stand for more than a few minutes without being overcome by dizziness.

She was eager to tell Justin, even though their conversations had become strained again. Sure, they communicated okay whenever it came to Sebastian, but when they were alone, they struggled to keep each other's gaze. Conversations were limited to casual chat about Justin's workday, new deals he was planning, what Jalissa was reading now, and what they were having for dinner.

But this was good news: she'd taken another huge leap toward wholeness, and she was eager to share it with him. So, she went looking for him, calling his name as she went. "Justin?"

She found him in his home office, standing at his desk with documents spread out before him, pen in hand, head bent, attention completely focused on his task. It almost made her smile to think that he was such an energetic man that sitting down made him antsy. He did most of his work standing, and even so he constantly vibrated with energy.

Jalissa had to call his name a second time before he heard her and looked up. She couldn't read the expression on his face, so she began to stammer out an apology for disturbing him. "Oh, I'm sorry. I didn't realize. It's nothing. I could come back."

He gave her a half smile. "No, it's fine." To demonstrate his willingness to listen, he placed the silver Mont Blanc pen down on the desk. "Talk to me."

Talk to you, she thought. *I'd love nothing better than to talk to you. But why is it always so hard?* It crossed her mind that maybe it was hard because what her body really wanted, she really wanted from him, had nothing to do with talking.

"Oh, I just wanted to tell you that my physio said she doesn't need to see me again for another month." She felt her face flush with pride. "I'm on my own now!"

Justin came out from behind the desk and stood in front of her. She could smell the subtle, masculine scent of his cologne, expensive and refined. It messed with her senses big time.

"That's great, Jalissa. I knew you could do it."

She nodded, pleased by his encouragement. "Now, if only my memory would begin to recover." It was so frustrating; she'd worked hard every day and managed to master her body, but still her mind was stubborn and insisted on lagging behind. Why? Wouldn't life be so much easier if she knew exactly who she was and was able to live within the context of both her past *and* her present?

He placed a comforting hand on her arm. "It's okay. I know it's hard. But give it time—"

"Justin!"

The voice in the doorway made them both spin around in surprise. Lorena was standing there, holding Seb in her arms, and her face was hot and red and angry. Her look grew even darker when she spotted Justin's hand on Jalissa's arm. The woman shot Jalissa such a scathing look that she instinctively took a step back. The glare was as violent as a punch.

"Yes?" Justin asked, his curiosity aroused. "Is everything okay with Seb?"

"No, it is not. Or, at least, it would not have been if I hadn't been there to intervene!"

A look of worry crossed his face. "What happened? Is he ill?" Quickly, he closed the space between himself and the nanny and took Seb into his arms, resting his hands against the baby's forehead and peering into his eyes.

"No, but he could have been hurt. He could have been worse, if I hadn't—"

"What is it, Lorena," Justin said impatiently. "I don't have time for games where my son is concerned. If something is wrong, spit it out."

Lorena flinched a little under the brunt of Justin's impatience, but then looked even more determined to tell her story. In fact, she began to preface it with great drama, enjoying the attention. "Well, as you know, he is crawling around a lot now. He will be on his feet and walking very soon. He will be all over the house." She threw Jalissa an evil look, one that she couldn't comprehend. "This is why we have the child-proof gates everywhere. This is why we keep the doors *closed.*"

"I know that," Justin answered impatiently.

In the past few weeks, Justin had become obsessed with safety, installing child-proof swing gates at strategic places, and tamper-proof devices on all cupboard and closet doors. He'd covered the electrical outlets months ago, even before Sebastian was navigating the floor on his own. He was a good dad, and safety was high on his list of priorities.

"Go on, Lorena," he said impatiently. "What is it?"

"I was in the kitchen, preparing Sebastian's lunch. I wasn't worried about him, because he was playing with his iguana just nearby. Then I looked around, and he was gone!" she paused dramatically, looking from Jalissa to Justin.

Jalissa felt an icy hand grasp the back of her neck. Had something really happened to her son? "And?" she demanded. "Where was he?"

Lorena acted as if she hadn't even spoken. As if she wasn't even in the room. "And do you know where he was?"

Justin's face and body radiated tension and anxiety. "Tell me now, Lorena. Goddammit, do you think I have time to wait?"

She waved her arm expansively in the direction of the garden. "Out there! Out there! In the driveway! Crawling toward the gate!"

57

Jalissa gasped in horror. That couldn't be possible. How could he have gotten out?

"What?" Justin roared. "My child was in the driveway? How could you have let this happen?"

"It wasn't my fault. He was with me, and safe. Everything was closed, as it should be, until the physiotherapist left."

Both Justin and Lorena turned to look at Jalissa. Her mouth fell open in horror. "You think I left the door open?"

Lorena stuck stubbornly by her story. "You let the physiotherapist out. I heard you open the door and tell her goodbye, but I didn't hear you close it."

"Of course, I closed it!" Jalissa responded angrily. "You think I'd be so irresponsible that I'd risk harm to my own child?"

When Justin turned to her, his face was stone, his eyes cold. "Are you sure you closed the door, Jalissa?"

"Of course, I did!" she protested. "I'm not an idiot!"

"Maybe it was that blow to your head," Lorena suggested insidiously. "Maybe it was your... you know, brain damage."

What the hell was this woman talking about? She stared in shock at Lorena's carefully innocent face and then turned to Justin. "Tell me you don't believe her, Justin!"

The man was cradling their son in his arms, holding him close and looking at Jalissa as if she had the potential to cause him harm. "We need to be extra careful in this phase in his development, Jalissa," he told her, as if she was some idiot schoolgirl who didn't know anything. "You're going to have to be very careful in everything you do. You need to double-check everything—"

"I closed the damn door! I did not let him get outside!" She took a step forward to examine the baby, and was horrified to notice that for just one second, Justin flinched away, as if he was afraid she'd try to take him. "Look at his romper! It's perfectly clean! Look at his knees and hands. If he was outside as she says, why isn't he dirty?"

"The grounds crew was here this morning, remember?" Lorena countered. "The entire driveway has been swept clear, and the blower has removed all the leaves and debris."

Jalissa glared at the nanny with murder in her eyes. The girl was lying, deliberately trying to make her look bad in Justin's eyes. But why?

"Thank you, Lorena," Justin said sincerely. "I'm glad you had the presence of mind to make sure he was safe."

Lorena practically glowed, throwing Jalissa a triumphant look that said, *Don't mess with me.* And that was when she finally understood. Lorena was in love with Justin. Not only that, but she saw Jalissa as competition, and was willing to stoop to lying to get her in trouble with him. She felt a cold sensation of dread creep up her spine. The woman was dangerous.

Justin was the father of her child, the man who'd pledged to look after Sebastian for the rest of his life, and he'd made this baby with her. By making love with *her.* What made this little nanny think she could turn up in this house and get between them? What made her think she could insinuate herself into this family and become a part of it?

Jalissa knew she'd made herself an enemy, but that was okay. From what everyone had told her, the old Jalissa never backed down from a fight. Well, the new Jalissa wouldn't either!

Justin was still talking nicely to Lorena, still oblivious to the nefarious woman's trickery. "Why don't you take the afternoon off, Lorena? You've sure earned it."

Lorena looked crestfallen. "I was kind of hoping to stick around for the rest of the day. You know..." She glared at Jalissa. "... to make sure he's safe."

Jalissa took a menacing step forward. "Now, look here you b—"

"It's fine, Lorena," Justin dismissed her. "That will be all."

Lorena *humphed* and spun around, stomped out of Justin's office and headed the way she'd come. For Jalissa, it was like watching a small, vicious predator- a ferret or no, a wolverine- slink back into its den.

She rounded on Justin. "Tell me you don't believe her!"

He tried to placate her. "It's easy to make a mistake, especially if you're fatigued from a grueling session."

"*I did not leave the door open!*" she yelled at him, so sharply that Sebastian looked startled.

Justin looked at her, surprised to hear her raise her voice. It was the first time she'd done so since she got here, and she didn't regret it. It was like a spark of the old her igniting. *Welcome back,* she thought to herself.

"Why would she make something like that up?" he asked calmly.

"Because she's in love with you." Jalissa said, shocked that he could have possibly missed the looks Lorena had been giving him.

He laughed scornfully. "That's ridiculous. She's a kid. Barely out of her teens."

"And does that make her more or less likely to be crushing on you hard?" Jalissa pointed out. She wanted to grab him by the shoulders and shake some sense into him. Jeez, men could be so dense sometimes!

He sighed, shifted the baby to his other shoulder, and looked weary of the argument. "Very well, Jalissa. But let's take every care to ensure Sebastian's safety in the future, okay?" As the baby began to drowse on his shoulder, Justin turned his attention back to the papers on his desk.

Jalissa felt deflated, disheartened and very angry. She knew she had been dismissed.

In the days that followed, it irked her to note that Justin had begun coming home a bit earlier, and was always willing to "help" her with basic caretaking duties, such as feeding or bathing their son. She knew that even though she had sworn her innocence, somewhere in the back of his head he was concerned that she might not be capable of ensuring Seb's safety.

Even though it was clear evidence of the tremendous love and care he felt for his son, his mistrust of her broke her heart. Meanwhile, Lorena kept swanning around, cooing at Sebastian and making inane baby talk with him, doubling down whenever Justin was within earshot.

And when he was out, it was a different story entirely. The house felt colder, darker, and Lorena did everything she could to make sure Jalissa had as little time with her son as possible: he was sleeping, he was eating, she was walking him in the garden. Most of the time she demanded that Lorena hand him over—he was, after all, *her* son. Other times, Lorena prevailed, and that irked her no end.

She knew this wasn't over. Not by a long shot.

Chapter 9

The call came in the middle of the night: Justin rolled over and looked at his smartphone. When he saw his father's ID, he sat up in bed. Nothing good ever happened at three in the morning.

He answered the phone. "Dad?" he said, realizing that his heart was in his mouth. "Is everything okay? Did something happen to mom?"

The voice on the other end, the voice that been a source of strength for him for years, hastened to reassure him. "She's fine, Justin. She's right here beside me." To prove him right, he heard his mother's voice in the background, "Hello, Son. I'm fine. We're fine."

"Then what—"

"There's been a fire at one of the restaurants," his father announced.

"*Our* restaurant?" he asked, trying to come to grips with the idea. He, his brother Finn and their father, owned and ran several restaurants in Ottawa; they were a thriving business, with fine dining establishments set up in well-respected communities, as well as five fast-food establishments. To hear that one of them had been damaged by fire was horrifying. "What happened?"

"We don't know yet, but it's pretty bad. The damage was extensive. It's going to take a lot of work to repair."

"Was it gas? A boiler? Electrical fire?"

"We don't know," his father repeated. "The fire department can't begin to carry out their investigation for a day or two, when everything cools. And then we'll have to assess the damage and bring in the insurance adjustors."

"I'll be there today." Usually, he spent most of his time in Ottawa, where he'd been raised and where his parents still lived. He even owned property there, although whenever he went back he usually returned to his childhood home so he could spend time with his parents, whom he missed dearly. Since Jalissa's accident, he'd found himself spending more and more time in Montreal until it eventually made sense to buy the house and put down some roots here.

"Have you called Finn?"

"I have. He's not happy about it. He wants to know how something like that could have happened."

"Is he coming over?"

"He says he and Tyler are neck-deep in a new deal, and he can't spare the time."

Figures, Justin thought. He loved his brother, but Finn had very little interest in the restaurant business, which of course left everything up to Justin. He tried not to feel resentful of the fact that even though he was the son who was sure to respond to this crisis, his parents had still phoned Finn first. It was a situation he didn't like, but one he'd grown accustomed to.

He threw off the covers and got out of bed, not even bothering to cover his nudity. "I'll start packing and see what I can do about getting a flight over."

"You don't have to," his father hedged, but Justin knew he was simply not trying to burden him too much. He could still hear the hope in his voice.

"I do have to," he insisted.

"Are you sure?" his father asked. "I mean, with all you have going on with Jalissa and Sebastian?"

This gave him just a moment's pause. He'd been going into the office almost every day, often for as much as twelve hours, leaving Jalissa to care for Sebastian—along with Lorena, of course. But this time, he would be away for days.

The incident with the open door still sat uneasily on his mind. He wanted to believe that Jalissa hadn't left the door open, but head trauma was a strange thing and it was clear that her memory had been affected. And maybe Lorena did have a tiny crush on him, but to suggest that the young woman would deliberately put Sebastian in harm's way—or, at least, lie about him being in harm's way—was ludicrous.

"She's got Lorena to help," he promised his dad. "It'll only be for a few days. Everything will be fine. You know I'd never leave you guys to deal with this alone."

The relief in his father's voice was palpable. "Thank you, Son." On a brighter note, he added, "Violet will be happy to see you."

"Of course she will," he joked, trying to lighten the mood. "Girls are always happy to see their big brother."

"Only by seven minutes," his mother announced in the background.

"That's good enough for me," he said, smiling into the phone, even though it wasn't a video call. He was always glad to see his parents and twin sister. "See you soon."

By the time the sun was up, he was already packed and booked on a flight to Ottawa. He knocked on Jalissa's bedroom door, but found it empty. On instinct, he went to Seb's room, where he found her standing at the crib, staring down at the small, sleeping form.

"Morning."

She jumped at the sound of his voice. He knew she was still mad at him over the open-door incident, but as much as he hated that, Sebastian's safety always came first, and he'd rather err on the side of caution than on the side of tragedy.

The smile she offered him was weak, but he appreciated the effort. "Good morning."

Justin came to stand next to her. "Was he fussy?"

She shook her head. "No, he's been a gem. Hasn't so much as made a murmur."

So, he realized, she'd gotten out of bed early just to stand at her son's side. *She's a good mom,* he reminded himself. *Maybe that whole thing* had *been a mistake.* He remembered he had some news for her; news she probably wouldn't like. "I have to fly to Ottawa this morning. To be with my folks."

"Why?" She stared at him in surprised concern, moving away from the crib so that their conversation didn't disturb Sebastian. "Are they okay?"

"They're fine, but there was a fire at one of the restaurants."

She looked horrified. "What kind of fire?"

"No idea." He began to walk out of the nursery, hoping she would follow, because he didn't want their voices to wake the baby up. "It'll take a few days for the investigators to come up with a source of the blaze."

He felt her fall into step with him. He didn't know why, but he found himself heading to the patio where the pale rays of the morning sun were just about chasing the mist away.

"Is that how long you'll be gone? A few days?"

He nodded without answering.

"And what about Seb?" Her eyes were focused on him, alert, trying to read his response.

"You guys will be fine. I can ask Lorena to sleep in, if you—"

"No!" she interrupted him hastily. "That's not necessary!"

"You'll need her support, Jalissa," he explained patiently. "Babies aren't easy to deal with, especially when they're crawling."

She flinched inwardly at the clear implication, but stood her ground. "Fine. If you want me to work with her, I will. But she does not need to sleep over. Sebastian is my son, and I can care for him. I'll keep the baby monitor in my room. If necessary, I'll sleep in the nursery. But please, just trust me."

He examined her eyes carefully and saw only sincerity. He gave her a slight smile. "That's fine, Jalissa. You'll do great."

The relief on her face was tremendous. "Thank you."

He wouldn't have time to wait for Lorena to arrive for duty, so as he assembled his bags at the front entrance to wait for the limousine to take him to the airport, he gave her a few quick instructions. Then he was off, confident that everything would be okay.

* * *

Both his parents met him at the airport, and he embraced them with great affection, even though he saw them regularly. He'd brought flowers for his mom and was armed with a silver photo album filled with Sebastian's most recent photos; some of them included Jalissa. As much as he was a man who embraced technology, he believed that baby pictures should always be in tangible form; it was as if they captured the image of the child and froze it in time for future enjoyment.

They first stopped at the restaurant, so Justin could have a look at the damage, which was extensive. The entrance and dining area were mostly unscathed, although the stench of smoke was so pervasive that the soft furnishings would have to be replaced, and the walls repainted. The expense would be great, and he could only hope that the insurance would cover most of it.

In the kitchen, the devastation was so extreme that all he could do was stop and look around himself in frank amazement. The ground was still sodden from the fire hoses, and clumps of white foam from the fire extinguishers had dried on the walls like melted marshmallow. The charred and blackened walls made it clear that the fire had been centered around the stoves and ovens, which wasn't surprising. But the question remained; how had it happened? Was it an accident? Negligence? Or a deliberate act of sabotage?

He noticed that his mother was close to tears. It hurt his heart, as he knew how much she and his dad had put into the business. He put his arms around her. "Come on, Mom. Let's get back to the house. We'll get working on fixing it up as soon as we can, okay?"

She nodded gratefully, and with her husband on one side and her son on the other, they walked back to the car.

Back at the family home, Justin enjoyed a cheerful meal with his parents. Afterward, he hurried to his childhood room, where he always slept when he visited, eager to get in touch with Jalissa and find out how Sebastian was doing.

She immediately picked up. "I know you aren't really calling for me," she joked, "but don't worry, Seb is as eager to talk to you as you are to talk to him."

"Of course I'm calling for you," he answered softly. "How are you?"

"Great."

"You look great."

She flushed and lifted Seb into her arms, angling the phone camera so he could see them both. "Say hi to Daddy, Seb," she coaxed.

Sebastian said no such thing, but he cooed at the camera in a way that made Justin feel as though he knew his dad was on the other end. It warmed Justin's heart. Mother and son were doing well; he knew he didn't have to worry too much about leaving them. He listened indulgently as Jalissa told him a story about trying to feed Seb boiled eggs at breakfast, but that *he* wound up trying to feed *her* by the squished handful.

"Generous kid," Justin observed.

"Like his dad." She smiled at him. "I'll be glad, *we'll* be glad when you're back."

"Me too," he confessed.

Chapter 10

J alissa clicked her phone off and slipped it into her pocket. It felt good to know that Justin had been thinking about them, that he missed them so much that he couldn't go half a day without getting in touch.

Well, maybe he *was* really calling to see Seb, but she'd live with that, for now. She walked Seb out of the nursery, enjoying the comforting weight of him in her arms, and then bumped directly into Lorena. "Sorry," she said instinctively. It irked her that Justin had insisted that this woman would have to come in to work every day and she would have to put up with her presence, but it was Justin's home and the nanny was his employee.

She made another attempt to get to the patio, but the nanny shifted her position, holding out her arms. "It's time for his dinner. Let me give it to him."

Jalissa turned her body sideways as if protecting Sebastian from a kidnapping. "I will give him his dinner."

"Are you sure?" the other woman asked placidly. "I mean, if you're tired, I can do it."

"I am not tired. I'm well rested, thank you. And *I* will feed *my son*."

Loud, elaborate sigh and exaggerated eye-roll from Lorena. "Very well. At this time of day, he normally eats pureed food—"

"I know that!" Jalissa snapped.

"There are bottles of baby food on the cupboard."

"I know that. I put them there." Lorena and her smug sense of superiority, and her constant hints that Jalissa was unable to care for her own child, were really getting on her nerves. Without another word, she marched to the cupboard, took down a small jar of pureed yams that was right up front, and armed herself with a teaspoon, a bib, and a baby bottle of water to wash it all down. Seb was eying the jar of food eagerly; he knew what was coming.

"You're a hungry little guy aren't you," Jalissa commented indulgently. "Don't worry. It's coming."

She sat him in his highchair, popped open the bottle, and began to feed him. One mouthful, and then two; he liked it so much she didn't even have to play 'airplane' to get him to open his mouth. As she was about to put the third spoonful into the baby's mouth, the food was slapped away, going flying onto the carpet and leaving a streak of brown mush that would be hard to clean up. Lorena was standing over the highchair, panting.

"What the—"

"That food is tainted!" Lorena announced, snatching up the baby bottle and holding the label out to her. "See?"

"That's not possible. I bought and stocked those bottles myself, only yesterday."

"Well, it's past its expiration date, see?" She waved the label on the bottle in front of Jalissa's face like a semaphore flag.

Jalissa couldn't believe what she was seeing. It was true; the Best By date was almost a week gone past. She looked in horror at Seb, who had thoroughly enjoyed the first two spoonsful, and was waiting eagerly for his next, mouth open like a little bird's. "I just bought these!" she insisted, confused. "And I checked the labels before I did so."

Lorena looked triumphant. "Well, maybe you made a mistake. You know, with your..." she pointed at Jalissa's head, "... injury."

"I did not... wait... how did you know the food was off?"

Lorena lifted her chin stubbornly. "I always check the labels. I take very good care of the little one..."

"But you came in here, already knowing that there was something wrong with it!"

"I did no such thing. I simply had a hunch, so I checked it. And my hunch was right. But I am afraid that it will be my duty to let Justin know what happened today. To ensure that Sebastian is protected from future mistakes."

Jalissa groaned in horrified realization. "You set me up! You did this! You put that old bottle up there, didn't you?"

"That's absurd."

"Why? Why would you do this? You'd risk getting a child sick just to make me look bad?"

Lorena looked mulish. "I have no idea what you're talking about." She folded her arms and looked away.

Jalissa decided she'd had enough. She took a menacing step toward the younger woman. "Listen to me. I don't know what kind of game you think you're playing, but you do not get to mess with the well-being of my child. Sebastian is *my* son and if you put him in jeopardy one more time, in any way, you will have me to contend with." She hated that she was shaking out of rage; something that the other woman might see as a sign of weakness.

"I will still have to report this to Justin," Lorena insisted.

"You do that and—"

"I will. He is my employer."

"Lorena, I promise you; if you breathe one word of this to Justin, I will see you packing your bags. Do you understand me?"

Lorena pinched her lips together and looked away.

Jalissa held Seb tightly against her chest, examining his face for any signs of being unwell. She was sure that a few days past expiration would do the baby no harm, and she'd be calling his pediatrician immediately to make sure, but in the meantime, "You can take the rest of the day off, Lorena, and tomorrow, too. Seb and I will be fine."

Lorena shook her head. "Sorry." She didn't look sorry at all. "*Justin* was the one who hired me. I work for *him*, not *you*. And I will remain here as long as my contract states. I will remain here until *he* says otherwise."

Much as she hated to admit it, Jalissa knew that she had been defeated for the time being. So, she said, "Fine. If you want to stay, stay. Eat, drink, watch a movie on Lifetime; I don't care. Do whatever suits your fancy until Justin comes back. Just stay away from me and my kid."

She went back to the kitchen, feeling both scared and angry. Clearly, this woman was unhinged, and would stop at nothing to rid herself of Jalissa and her perceived competition for Justin and Seb's affections. It was crazy! But unless she could convince Justin of that fact, she'd better watch her back and keep an alert eye on Sebastian's well-being and safety. She couldn't afford any other mishaps where he was concerned.

* * *

"Hey, Big Guy."

Justin looked up to see his twin, Violet, standing in the doorway of their parent's sunroom where he had been relaxing in an easy chair, engrossed in the financial section of *The Globe and Mail*. She'd had a late workday and hadn't been able to make it back in time for the family dinner, and it was obvious that she was excited to see him.

"Hey, Baby Sister," he answered, carefully folding the paper and putting it aside before standing up to give her a hug. A rush of happiness went through him; his sister always had that effect on him. He lifted her off the ground, twirled her around once, and then, when she started punching him in the shoulder, he set her down again. They stood there for several moments, grinning at each other like idiots.

"Good to see you," she finally said.

"Good to see you, too. Are you gaining weight?"

She slapped him, hard. "Shut up!"

Violet was as much of a health nut as he was and hit the gym at least five times a week. The idea of her gaining weight was ridiculous. But for a year or two in their early teens she had been a bit chubby, and he knew that the mention of that pudge was a great way to be a brotherly pain in the butt.

She walked to the maple-wood drinks cabinet in the corner and began rooting around. "Looks like the folks have a decent-looking bottle of 12-Year-Old Scotch in here. Join me for a sip?"

"Sure." He got down two whiskey glasses and filled them with ice, holding them out while Violet poured them each a measure. Then he followed his sister back to the seating area, opting to share the couch with her rather than to reprise his former position in the easy chair. "So what's up with you?" he asked. "You dating?"

"Meh," she said dismissively. "Nothing worth going on about. I was seeing someone nice for a while, but she migrated to Spain. I'm more interested in *your* life. How's my nephew? Studying for his MBA yet?"

He laughed. "Well, he's started crawling around and holding on to furniture to stand up."

"So, a little while longer 'till college then," she giggled.

Justin loved the sound of his sister's laughter. It made him feel so connected, so grounded, especially in times of upheaval.

"Is he eating solid food yet?"

"Sure is."

"And what about Jalissa?"

"She's eating solid food, too," he answered flippantly.

"You know that's not what I mean," she chided him.

He sobered up a little. "I know." Then he stared pensively into his drink, momentarily engrossed in the swirling patterns his ice cubes made in the glass.

Violet refused to let him go that easily. "How's she settling in with the knowledge that you two have a baby together?"

"It was a huge shock at first," he answered truthfully. "But that's only normal, right? I mean, it's not every day you wake up after having been asleep almost as long as Sleeping Beauty, to find out you're a mom!"

Violet nodded in emphatic agreement.

Justin went on, "But she settled in right away. They took to each other immediately, and she learned fast, you know, the basics. How to change a diaper, how to warm up a bottle. And this is on top of all her other challenges, learning to master her own body again, after coming out of that coma. She was really brave, and I'm proud of her."

"So you think she's open to being his mother long term?"

He paused awhile before he answered. "There's no doubt in my mind that she loves him, and he loves her. Call it maternal instinct or whatever. But she cares about him and wants him to thrive. She would never allow him to come to any harm." The moment those words came out of his lips, his mind flew back to the incident with the open front door. No, he decided, there was no way Jalissa would have been that careless. Surely there'd been a misunderstanding. Maybe, for some reason, the lock on the door had popped? He would check on it when he got home.

"What about the two of you?" Violet's voice interrupted his thoughts. "You two getting along?"

He thought about their kiss and felt his face go hot. "Given the circumstances, I think we're doing okay. We could be better, but—"

"You mean she hasn't fallen for the Tremblay charm as easily as she did the last time?" Violet teased.

"I guess not," he answered ruefully. He remembered the way it had felt to kiss her, to hold her close and feel her body grow warm and pliant under his. To feel his need rise within him and for her body to answer his call. He knew he was flushing, because Violet gave him a triumphant smile.

"You're in love with her."

"That's what Finn said. What is it with you two?" he asked irritably.

The surprise on his sister's face made him realize he'd made a big mistake. "You're engaged, Justin. You were planning to get married and raise your child together. And after her accident, you were there for her, fighting for her life and the life of your baby. You want to tell me that's not love?"

There it was again, that lie about the engagement. He'd known from the moment it had left his lips a year and a half ago that it would have come back to bite him in the ass, but it had all been worth the risk. He hated being untruthful with his sister, but he answered lamely, "Well, it's not that. It's just with all that's happened, and after all this time, it's been hard to reconnect. Hard to find what we'd had before her accident. Especially since she doesn't remember our relationship."

"You two aren't sleeping together yet?"

As if, he thought. "I don't think she's ready for that yet. Physically or emotionally."

"And once she's strong enough, once she's ready, do you think she'll want to?"

Again, there was the memory of Jalissa's kiss, and the flashing images of the looks she often gave him, many of which he couldn't interpret, but a few he knew in his heart were curiosity and desire. He couldn't bring himself to answer.

Violet downed the last of her drink, and in a twin-like echo, he followed suit. Their empty glasses sat side by side on the coffee table in front of them.

He recognized the look on Violet's face and knew at once that she was on the warpath. When she had an idea in her head, she didn't give up.

"Brother, have you considered that it would help Jalissa get her memory back if you tell her what really happened that night? Before she rushed out into the night and had her accident?"

He winced. His memories of that night were so clear that it was as if he'd slipped back along the space-time continuum and was there again, in his original Montreal apartment, in the living room, having a raging fight with Jalissa. About him and her, about their baby. About her never wanting anything to do with him again. "I want no ties at all!" she'd screamed at him.

He remembered her storming around, so enraged that she couldn't even find her backpack or the keys to her motorbike. He remembered grasping her by the arm, clad in her usual tight-fitting leather biker's jacket and pants, begging her to calm down and think for a minute. "Think about it," he'd begged. "It's not just about us anymore."

But the old Jalissa, tempestuous and reckless, hadn't even spared him a few seconds to plead his case. She'd located those damn keys, wrenched her arm from his grasp, stormed down his driveway and hopped onto her cherry-red Kawasaki. Then zoomed out into the road to meet her appointment with destiny.

He wondered what would have happened if he'd forcibly held her back, if only for a moment. If he'd kept her from leaving, pleaded with her one more time to listen, to hear him out. Would things have been different? Would the accident not have happened?

And if it hadn't, where would they be now? He, Jalissa and—most importantly—Seb?

Violet knew him well enough not to interrupt his thoughts, but waited until the thoughts that chased each other across his face came to settle.

"I don't know," he finally admitted. "I don't know if telling her about everything would be in her best interest."

"Is it that? Or is it that *not* telling her is in *your* best interest?"

He felt his shoulders slump. "God, Vi, you're an astute little wench."

"Huh. We think alike. Did you really not expect me to know what's going on in your head?" Then she patted his cheek and gave her trademark smile, a beautiful, feminine version of his own. "I'm not going to torment you anymore, Big Brother. Let's drop it, okay?"

"Okay," he said gratefully.

"And since our parents were kind enough to provide this exemplary bottle of Scotch for our consumption, what do you say we make the best use of it? Maybe we could watch a movie." She picked up the TV remote, turned it on, and started clicking.

Justin poured them each another shot and then carefully put the bottle away. It wouldn't do any good to let stress cause him to overdo it. "I'll watch a movie with you on one condition."

"What's that?" she answered, not looking up, still clicking.

"That you don't torment me with any of your ghastly rom-coms."

She pretended to be outraged. "Rom-coms? Me? Give me a good slasher movie any day."

"That sounds more like it," he agreed, and settled in next to her.

Chapter 11

J alissa was surprised to discover that she had no need for a recipe. The duck meat was marinating in a blend of Dijon mustard and white wine. It would be ready to sauté in half an hour. The portobello mushrooms for the risotto were plump and fresh, and as she set about slicing them, she felt a vaguely familiar sense of excitement. The kitchen had become a place of quiet pleasure for her, where she'd begun to challenge herself day by day. She remembered finding the array of fine, expensive cooking implements and pots among her possessions in the storage container. She could sense that deep in her chest beat the heart of a great cook. The problem was that she couldn't remember any of it. Not working as a chef, not going to culinary school, nothing.

There was the sound of a limo pulling up in the driveway, and she raced to the window to look out. Her heart beat double time when she realized it was Justin, back from his trip to his family in Ottawa. Glancing at the clock, Jalissa noted that he was more than an hour early. She'd been hoping to greet him with a fully cooked meal, but she was glad he was here. Smoothing down her apron and quickly making sure her hair was in place, she hurried to the door.

Look at me, she thought, *getting all flustered! What is this man doing to me?*

She put her hand on the doorknob at the same time he did, and there was a funny bit of push-and-pull before it opened. There he was, tall and handsome, and she had to resist the urge to throw her arms around him and welcome him home. Instead, she stood there, grinning idiotically, until it occurred to her that maybe she should step aside and let him in.

"Hi." He smiled down at her.

"Hi, Justin." She smiled back.

He glanced around. "Where's Seb? Is he okay?"

Was there was a note of worry in his voice? Was he was concerned that she hadn't been taking care of him properly? "He's fine," she said firmly. "He's upstairs with the nanny." She couldn't bring herself to voice that treacherous woman's name. Over the past couple of days, the two of them steadfastly avoided each other, meeting only to exchange custody of Sebastian. Jalissa had insisted that all practicalities, from bathing to feeding to changing diapers, were her job. She only relinquished him at times like these, when she was in the kitchen, which was clearly a dangerous place for a crawling child.

"I'll go say hi." He held up a large package. "I got him a gift."

The package was bulky and awkwardly wrapped, but even so, she could see what it was. "You bought him a *drum?* Did you also buy earplugs for us?" she joked.

"Remind me to pick up a few pairs in the morning," he joked back, heading inside and loosening his tie as he did so.

Jalissa returned to the kitchen and busied herself. She got the meat going and then started on the risotto. When Justin came back, he had showered, and in the place of his business suit, was wearing well-worn jeans and a light gray polo shirt that set off his eyes. He drifted into the kitchen, sniffing the air. "Something smells amazing. Did you have dinner delivered?"

She punched him on the arm. "Delivery? I've been slaving away at making you a top-notch dinner, you beast!"

Instead of smiling, he looked concerned. "Have you really? Do you think that's okay for you to do? Are you tired? Are you dizzy?"

She loved that he was concerned for her, but she didn't want him getting over-protective. "I'm fine."

"Let me do it. Pull up a chair and I'll finish."

"I'm fine, Justin!" she insisted. "It's been two months since I woke up. I'm getting stronger every day. Let me do this."

He reached for a chef's knife and held it in an almost cartoonish 'I'm ready' pose. "Okay, but I get to help. What are we making?"

Proudly, Jalissa led him through the dishes one by one. "*Canard à la moutarde à l'ancienne,* portobello risotto, petit pois, and a wilted-spinach salad."

His brows shot up. "Duck? That's a rarity. Is it a special occasion? I *know* I didn't forget your birthday."

The implied compliment made her flush. "No, I just wanted to make you something nice."

He looked at her for so long that she felt a fluttering in the pit of her stomach. "Nice." Moving to her side, he took a deep inhale. "That duck smells like heaven!"

"The secret is a little of honey in the marinade. Not much, just a *soupçon.* That's what my grandmother always told me." She paused, stopping dead, fingers clasped around a large spatula, as the full impact of her words hit home. *My grandmother,* she'd said. She'd remembered her grandmother's words!

"Justin!" she squealed. "I remembered!"

For a moment, she could have sworn he paled. "What did you remember?"

"My grandmother's recipe for duck! I mean, I remember that this recipe is hers! Isn't that amazing?" In her delight, she threw herself into his arms. He was taken aback for a second, but then his arms closed around her waist, and he held her close. He felt so good. He smelled so good. She discovered that she was lifting up on tiptoe, pressing her lips against his, and he was kissing her back, first tentatively, then deeply. After days apart, the contact almost shorted out her brain. She parted her lips, inviting him in. Then the realization of what she was doing dragged her back to her senses, and she pulled away. Her breathing was ragged, and she could have sworn that the kitchen had gotten way hotter. Without saying another word about the kiss, or even acknowledging it had happened, she laid out the ingredients for the salad and handed him a large crystal salad bowl. "All yours," she said abruptly.

By tacit agreement, they went to work side by side. Needing to fill the void, she asked him about the trip, and he began telling her of the sorry state of the family's restaurant and the badly burned kitchen. "They think it's arson," he said. "But we can't figure out who or why. It's driving me crazy. I feel so bad about it."

"Why do you feel bad?"

"Because of how it will affect the employees. If only I'd known. If only there was a way to have prevented it from happening."

Jalissa stopped her chopping, set down her knife, and turned to face him. "You can't blame yourself for everything that happens, Justin. You can't carry so much guilt around. It will weigh down your soul."

"Guilt," he murmured, more to himself than to her. "Huh."

What did he mean by that, she wondered—and what exactly was he referring to?

* * *

Justin eased the car into 'park' outside his brother's house, noticing as he did so that Tyler and Kaiya were already there. He was almost reluctant to go inside, because it meant that he would have to release Jalissa's hand, which was lightly resting on his thigh and had been for most of the drive over. Her hand felt so warm in his, and the contact with her skin so fulfilling that he was afraid that if he let her go, he might break the spell that had surrounded them in the few days since he returned from Ottawa.

The last few evenings had been so comfortable that he was reluctant to leave for work in the morning and eager to get back home when the day's work was done. It was as if that evening they'd shared in the kitchen had opened up a new doorway for Jalissa and him, and they had wandered through it.

In that spontaneous moment, she'd thrown her arms around him and kissed him, and he knew that the connection between them was real. He'd felt it, and so had she. He had taken to coming home as early as he could, and dismissing Lorena earlier than usual so that he and Jalissa could see about the task of caring for Seb together. Lorena looked none too happy about that, so he was certain to let her know that her salary wouldn't be affected.

The past few evenings had been spent in comfortable familiarity; together they made dinner, ate, fed Sebastian, and settled in his nursery to read him a bedtime story. As soon as he was asleep, which was usually quite quick, bless him, they went out to the living room and sat side by side on the couch to watch a little TV. Sometimes the news, sometimes a gory horror movie, which he discovered Jalissa loved. Often, she would lay her head against his shoulder. Oftentimes, when he bent forward to kiss her lightly, she kissed him back.

He couldn't be happier.

He looked down at her in admiration as he reached over and unbuckled her seatbelt; her knee-length wool dress was a deep burgundy, trimmed with pewter buttons, conservative yet sexy. Only Jalissa could make such a thing possible. "You look amazing tonight," he said softly.

She beamed.

Without another word, he pressed a soft kiss against her cheek, and then exited the vehicle. He walked quickly around to the other door and opened it, then reached in the back to extricate Sebastian from his car seat. He had dozed off on the way over, but seemed to sense the excitement and was instantly awake.

Finn and Kalilah greeted them at the door with enthusiastic hugs and kisses. Justin threw an admiring glance at Kalilah; she was barely showing now, but they were right when they said that pregnancy could leave a glow on a woman's face. She looked happy and in love, both with his brother and with her role as a mom. He wondered what Jalissa would have been like if she had been conscious during her pregnancy.

The other couple was waiting for them at the table, with a stack of board game boxes piled high. It was game night, and although Justin wasn't exactly a team player, he looked forward to the intense competition and camaraderie. Besides, the games were seldom finished; usually game night degenerated into an evening of good food and wine, gossip and conversation.

They decided that Pictionary was the order of the evening, and while Kalilah's eldest daughter, Lili, eagerly took charge of Seb, they got down to some serious playtime. Justin listened as Jalissa gleefully recounted her experience with remembering her grandmother's recipe for duck. While the others shared their excitement, he brooded, not sure that he was as happy as they were. He knew it was selfish—he even hated himself for it—but the fact that Jalissa's memory was slowly seeping back into her consciousness was a threat to the fragile domestic happiness he'd managed to create with her and their son.

What would happen when Jalissa found out that he had lied to her?

"Justin!" Kaiya chided him. "Are you paying attention? I drew you a perfectly good frying pan, and you let the timer run out!" She was his Pictionary partner tonight, as they'd split up the couples to eliminate the unfair advantage of husbands and wives reading each other's minds through that psychic connection couples seemed to develop.

He realized he'd been sulking, and in his inattention, he'd lost his team a point. "Sorry, partner. I'll do better next time."

She chucked a pistachio at him, hitting him square in the forehead. "You'd better!"

One of the hints was 'baby carriage', which, of course, sent the women into a flurry of conversation about Kalilah's pregnancy. "I hope you're keeping a pregnancy journal," her sister warned her.

"Of course! I'm jotting down every little detail. I'm even gluing little mementos into the pages, like the first ultrasounds."

"Have you taped down your pregnancy test?" Kaiya laughed, and a collective response of "Ewwww!" went around the table.

"What!" she huffed jokingly. "Taking your pregnancy test is a great experience! Worthy of preserving!"

"Not if you're just a teenager," Jalissa piped up. "Do you remember when you found out you were pregnant with Lilianna? You thought *I* was the pregnant one. I brought home, like, ten tests, and we went through all of them. You only took one because you didn't want me to do it alone." She took another sip of her chardonnay and laughed. "Turns out, you were the one who..." She trailed off, realizing that everyone was staring at her. "What?"

"You remember that?" Kaiya asked softly.

"Of course," Jalissa scoffed. "Why wouldn't..." She clapped a hand over her mouth. She'd remembered something that happened almost ten years ago!

Of one accord, the two sisters leaped up and threw their arms around her, making such a racket with their excited squeals that the kids in the adjacent room stopped playing with their toys and stared.

"You remember! You remember!" Kaiya enthused. "What else?"

Jalissa frowned, as if trying to reach into her memory like a diver piercing the darkness of the deep sea, below the level where the sun could reach. Justin realized he was holding his breath.

"I remember how mad your parents were. How they sent you away to... Nova Scotia? No." She snapped her fingers, urging the memory to come to her. "It was New Brunswick! You had your baby there...." She paused, glancing past Tyler's shoulder and seeming to notice that Lili was watching and listening. She finished in a hushed voice, "And I remember what happened after that."

There were more gleeful hurrahs, and Jalissa turned to Justin, seeking affirmation. "It's coming back to me!"

Justin knew he should be happy for Jalissa. He wanted more than anything for her to get better, but he also knew what could happen if she became fully aware of everything that had transpired between them. *Oh, God*, he thought.

But he forced a smile onto his lips and hugged her tightly. "That's great, Babe. I'm so proud of you."

She seemed to sense that something was off in his response, because her dark eyes searched his, but she didn't say anything.

Finn leaped up. "This calls for a celebration! I have a bottle of Moët that's been waiting for exactly this moment." As he disappeared from the room in search of the precious bottle, Justin realized that the last thing he wanted was a celebratory drink.

"You okay?" Jalissa asked with concern.

"I'm great," he assured while doing his best to fake a smile. "I just need some air, that's all."

"Want me to come?"

"No," Justin insisted, "It's fine." After giving Jalissa's shoulder a light squeeze, he slipped outside without stopping to put on his jacket. Justin immediately felt the chill settle over him. The mild shock was bracing, and he gulped it in, enjoying the burning in his lungs. He didn't know what bothered him more; Jalissa getting all her memories back or the fact that Jalissa remembered things about everyone else except him.

He needed to think.

Chapter 12

The ride home was solemn. Jalissa felt deflated, let down. She'd been so excited by the recent flashes of memory, a sure indication that she was on the mend. And yet, Justin didn't seem to share her joy.

The rest of the night had been a little muted; as if everyone had subconsciously noted a shift in the atmosphere. Instead of segueing from Pictionary to Scrabble or Trivial Pursuit, they'd decided to call it a night.

Seb was asleep even before his father buckled him into the car seat, so his parents spoke softly on the way home. They talked about nothing in particular - upcoming hockey games and ideas for Seb's birthday party.

Together, they put the baby to bed; no need for bedtime stories, as Seb was out cold. Once they'd quietly exited the nursery and closed the door, Justin and Jalissa stood in the hall looking at each other. Jalissa's head was full of questions: *What was going on? Why was he so quiet?*

But instead of addressing the sudden awkwardness, Justin took her into his arms, kissed her tenderly on the lips, and then stroked her cheek. "I'm proud of you, Sweetheart," he murmured. Then they separated and went to their respective rooms.

That night, Jalissa couldn't seem to find a comfortable position in the bed; eventually succumbing to exhaustion around four in the morning. When she woke up, it was well past ten and she'd missed the chance to give Sebastian his breakfast. Cursing the lost opportunity, Jalissa hurriedly cleaned up and went looking for her son.

She found him in the sun room, in the company of the detestable Lorena, who had, in her opinion, dressed him inappropriately to play indoors. The poor boy was wearing so many layers of clothing that he looked like a fragile glass ornament wadded up in cotton wool. Jalissa considered saying something, but the nanny gave her a sour look and gathered Seb up into her arms, encircling him like a mama python protecting her egg. So instead, Jalissa rolled her eyes and went in search of Justin.

Whenever her buried memories were mentioned Jalissa sensed that Justin was keeping some secret from her. Enough was enough. She would have it out with him now. When she found him, he was in his office frowning down at a stack of papers, though he didn't seem entirely focused on them. A deep breath and she pushed the door shut.

"I need to talk with you," she announced; her voice as firm as she could manage.

His beautiful eyes darkened as they met hers. Justin tidied his paperwork, pushed it aside and stood, shoulders squared as if preparing himself for their discussion.

Pushing away from the door, Jalissa strode around the desk to face him, her head tilted back so she could meet his gaze evenly. She was to not backing down. "I need you to spit it out. Whatever it is." As he inhaled to respond, she held up a hand. "And don't try to act like you don't know what I'm talking about. That's beneath you. I want the truth, Justin."

Even with her eyes on his face, Jalissa noted the fingers of his left-hand drumming against the thigh of his trousers. "Okay, Sweetheart."

Oh, how it killed her when he called her that!

"The truth is that I'm a coward. I care about you deeply, and I want nothing more for you to recover fully. And yet—"

"And yet?" she demanded.

Justin held her gaze, resolute. "And yet deep down I've been afraid of what would happen if you ever fully remembered the last time we spoke before your accident. Because I don't know how you'd react."

She folded her arms, partly to steady herself and partly to convey her determination. "Try me."

"The night you had that accident, you and I had a huge fight. A horrible, horrible fight."

Having already figured as much, Jalissa waited for the rest.

"We fought because you told me you were pregnant... and that you didn't want to be. You insisted that you never wanted children and that you'd told me so from the start—which you had. I knew that what we had between us was supposed to be just casual fun, just good sex and good company, but the moment I heard that I was going to be a father I was overjoyed."

"I didn't want the baby?" she repeated slowly, trying to let his words sink in. "I didn't want our child?"

Justin flinched slightly, then nodded. "You said that you'd have a termination before the week was out. The more I pleaded, the angrier you got."

Horror filled Jalissa's heart and her eyes began to burn. "I would never—"

He placed a hand on her arm. "*Cherie*, you shouted that you and I were through, that you never wanted to see me again, and that my being a father to your child wasn't an option. That once you walked out the door, I could forget about you and the pregnancy."

Tears stung like acid as they slid down her cheeks like lava. Sebastian's face came to her mind; sweet and angelic, with that unruly curly hair so much like her own, and that engaging smile, so much like his father's. "There was no way. No way..."

But she knew he was telling the truth. Jalissa had gotten the message loud and clear that she was much different from the woman she had been before the accident. With this revelation it was clear to her that she didn't like that harsh, selfish woman very much. "Why didn't you tell me, Justin? Why keep it a secret?"

When he didn't answer, she lunged at him, her fists hammering against his chest as anger overtook her grief. "You lying bastard! You kept this from me! How could you?"

Justin grabbed her flailing hands and held them fast. "Okay, I could have told you. But what would it achieve? You were doing so well— discovering yourself, getting back on your feet. I was afraid that if you knew, it would set you back. I didn't want you to hate yourself, especially not after you'd come to know and love Sebastian. I didn't want to put you in a position where you wouldn't be able to forgive yourself or me for what you intended to do."

Involuntarily, her head turned in the direction of the nursery, where Sebastian was playing—albeit bundled up like an Eskimo by that lunatic. And that's when she understood. Justin had lied, at least, by omission, to protect her. The pain she felt now at the revelation was nothing compared to what it would have felt like if she'd been presented with the news weeks ago, when she was, literally, trying to find her footing.

She breathed in deeply, trying to regain control. Maybe she'd flown off the handle there. She looked down at her hands, hardly believing she'd smacked him. Was that another example of her former self's fiery nature? "I... thank you," she murmured.

His brows shot up, as if that was the last thing he'd been expecting her to say.

"You were trying to protect me," she clarified. "And I'm..." she wanted to say, *so in love with you because of it,* but instead she said, "grateful."

Unable to stop herself, Jalissa reached up and wrapped her arms around Justin's neck and pulled him down. It was meant to be a hug, but the press of his body to hers and the feel of him changed to something more. She tipped back her head and angled his head down to hers, connecting their lips. Immediately, she was assailed by a wild desire for him; the slow simmer that had been on the back burner all this time had been turned up to high.

The taste of his mouth drove her crazy; the smell of him, even more so. When he tried to lift his head, she grasped his crisp dark hair and held on tight. She was willing to fight him on that! But he laughed softly into her mouth and lifted his head anyway, to look her in the eyes.

"Relax, I only wanted to do this."

He began nuzzling at her ear, grasping her gold hoop earring with his teeth and tugging on it. It should have been painful, but instead it made her gasp with pleasure. Justin continued, outlining her ear with the tip of his tongue, inflicting cruel bites as he went along. "You used to love this," he informed her.

"I still do," she panted. Standing on her toes, Jalissa pressed herself against him, enjoying the solid strength of his chest. A solidity echoed by the hardness below; an insistent ridge that was prodding her abdomen. Damn, she wished they were lying down! So, did he, it seemed.

With nimble fingers, Justin unbuttoned her blouse, slipping his hands inside to cup her breasts. They felt so right; like they belonged there.

She thanked whatever angel had whispered in her ear that she should buy bras that snapped in front. In her formerly weakened state, they had been easier for her to open and close. Now they presented the opportunity for Justin to gain access to her breasts, which, by now, were so sensitive that his merest touch made her breath hitch.

When he leaned forward and sucked one dark, chocolatey nipple into his mouth, grasping it between his teeth, she yowled. "You're... evil..." she managed to gasp.

"I know."

One hand slid down her hips, to the hem of her skirt, inching it up until his fingers encountered the damp crotch of her panties. With a cruel smile he began to rub her there, back and forth, not bothering to start slowly, but assaulting her senses and wrecking her willpower with a knowing touch and quick tempo.

"Justin..."

"Hmm?"

"If you don't make love to me right now..."

Laughter made Justin's chest rumble, and Jalissa wanted to growl in frustration. Suddenly he spun her around, so that she faced his desk. His hand still between her legs, still rubbing. She knew she'd be there in seconds. The stiff ridge pressing against her bottom was driving her mad. If he didn't yank down her panties and slip it inside her right now—

The door opened.

"Justin, Seb's taking his nap. I was wondering—"

Jalissa and Justin froze, caught in an explicit tableau that would haunt her dreams and Lorena stood there, taking it all in.

Quick thinking on Justin's part had Jalissa facing the wall opposite the door, giving her time to fix her bra and blouse. She did so with trembling hands before turning back to defiantly look the younger woman in the eye.

Why was Lorena still standing there? Jalissa wondered. *Shouldn't she be apologizing and walking away, to allow her employer time to make himself decent?* Instead, Lorena remained motionless, her face flushed purple, glaring daggers at Jalissa, who hurriedly pulled down her skirt and glared back.

Justin was equally perturbed, but at least had the presence of mind to say firmly, "Leave us, Lorena. And take the rest of the day off."

The door closed, but not before Lorena hurled a look at her that was so toxic it could whither flowers. When the woman was gone, Jalissa felt limp with relief and hot with embarrassment.

"You okay?"

Dragging her eyes from the door, Jalissa found Justin carefully studying her face. She nodded, not trusting herself to speak.

"I'm sorry about that." The brush of his lips against her ear sent shivers through her body, then he growled, "Mark my words; this isn't over."

Chapter 13

The oversized hall rang with the combined shouts and squeals of two hundred children laughing and playing. Jalissa was pretty sure she'd never been to a Fun Zone, so she was spinning like a top, gaping at all the booths, computer games, rids and activities.

Kaiya was appointed "keeper of the tokens" by Lili, who ran from game to game, crazy with excitement, while the adults, with TJ and Seb in their prams, tried to keep up. The babies were a tad too young for most of the games, but they sure enjoyed the carousels and mechanical pony rides.

The women were having an enlightening conversation, with Kaiya recounting amusing tales from their teen years, when the two best friends had gotten up to so much mischief. Like the time they sneaked into the Home Economics kitchen and replaced the granulated sugar with fine salt before the lesson on baking a pound cake. "It's a wonder I still went on to love cooking after that," Jalissa mused.

It made her so happy that Kaiya was taking the time to fill her in on these little snippets of her youth, which probably would never come back. It was all a part of her journey toward finding her true self. And after Justin's devastating revelation about wanting to end her pregnancy, she was glad to discover aspects of her old personality that were fun and likeable.

"You know you're glowing, right?" Kaiya pointed out.

Jalissa felt her face go hot. "Oh, am I?" she said with intense casualness.

"*Oh, am I?*" Kaiya mimicked. "It's all over your face. You and Justin must be getting along really well. Tell me." She leaned in closer, "have you slept with him yet?"

"No!" Jalissa momentarily scandalized before a grin burst forth. "Not exactly. Not yet, anyway. Although we might have, if it hadn't been for Evil Nanny." Quickly, she recounted the awkward, embarrassing encounter with Lorena in Justin's home office, while Kaiya howled.

"Nooo!"

"Yesss," she assured regretfully. "I don't know what it would take for Justin to wake up and realize that that woman wants him for herself. And will stop at nothing to get him."

Kaiya scoffed. "Oh, that's a laugh. That man has eyes only for you."

A wave of pleasure washed over Jalissa. She was ready to confide in her friend how close and tender things had become between them, and how hopeful she was beginning to feel about their future together. As she parted her lips to speak, a masculine voice behind her interrupted.

"Jalissa?"

She spun around to see a tall, good looking man with a neat beard and long black hair pulled back in a ponytail, smiling at her. His First People's heritage was evident in the tilt of his dark eyes, his glowing skin and sharp cheekbones. She immediately thought, *What a nice-looking guy.* And he was staring at her in a way that made her wonder how well she'd known him.

"It's Eric," he said, stepping a little closer. "Don't you remember me?" The idea that she didn't remember seemed to hurt.

Before she could answer, Kaiya stepped in. "Jalissa had an accident a year and a half ago, Eric. She's lost her memory."

"Oh," he said, still looking at her curiously.

Jalissa was burning to know. "Did we know each other?"

He gave her a rueful look. "We did. We dated for a while." And then, as if he didn't want to go down that painful road, he ushered forward the two little girls who had been lingering behind him, clinging to his pants legs. "These are my daughters, Anna and Erica. Say hello, girls."

The girls waved shyly and hid their faces against their father's thighs. In response, Jalissa indicated the two sleeping babies. "This is Kaiya's son, TJ, and mine, Sebastian. Over there, on the pinball machine, is her daughter, Lili—"

89

Eric cut her off with a gasp of amazement. "You have a child?"

She looked at him, perturbed by the extent of his surprise. "Yes. He's almost a year old—"

"Wow. I wouldn't have thought. You were always adamant about not..." He stopped, looking as if he'd said too much, then gave her a stilted smile. "Well, it was good seeing you. Both of you." Hastily, he gathered his two little girls and hurried away.

Jalissa turned to Kaiya, puzzled and hurt. "What was that all about?"

Kaiya contemplated her answer before saying, "You dated for about nine months. Things were going pretty well for you two. He was in love with you and he even proposed a few times, but you never accepted. You said you two wanted different things... I believe you had a deep fondness for him too."

There it was again, she thought. Why, why, why was the old Jalissa against having children? Was that even possible? She could tell there was more to the story, which Kaiya seemed reluctant to tell her, so she waited pointedly.

"And you cheated on him," Kaiya blurted. "That's why he ended it."

"Me? Cheated?"

Kaiya said nothing.

Jalissa plopped down into one of the brightly colored plastic chairs, suddenly feeling weak. "Do I want to know with whom?"

"Spare yourself from the unnecessary information," Kaiya advised.

Taking a deep breath, she asked, "Kaiya? How many men have I had sex with?"

Her friend looked at her and bit on her lip. She knew that Kaiya did this when she was nervous.

"Lissa, it doesn't matter."

"It matters to me," she retorted.

"Alright, alright. Do you want all of it or just the ones you considered were even worth mentioning? You did have a few you un-fucked."

"Un-fucked?"

"Yes. If the sex was horrible, you simply didn't count them as a worthy sex partner." Her friend shrugged and Jalissa cringed.

"Tell me all of it." And Kaiya did. Mentioning every single person Jalissa had sex with.

She stared down into her melted slushie, which now seemed disgusting to her. "Who was that person? Who was I? A woman who hated children. Who wanted to have an abortion rather than give birth to this wonderful miracle of a baby? Who cheated, lied and was overly promiscuous. Who was I?"

Kaiya's hand closed around hers and gave a reassuring, friendly squeeze. "Don't be too hard on yourself, Lissa. We all did stupid things in the past, but you have your entire future ahead of you. Thank God for a fresh start."

* * *

"It's okay," Justin said. They were sitting in the living room, in front of the giant bay windows, looking out into the bright evening sky. He'd listened patiently to Jalissa's story of her encounter with the man called Eric at the Fun Zone earlier, and it hurt him to see how distressed it had made her. "The past is in the past, *Cherie.*"

"That's exactly what Kaiya said!" she wailed in frustration.

"Then believe her," he advised with a smile. He slipped his arm around her waist and turned her to face him. "You have the opportunity to build a whole new you from the ground up. Not many people get that chance."

"How do *you* feel about the old me?" She looked at him, and in her eyes Justin saw a plea for the reassurance that she had been—and still was—a good person.

He stroked her cheek and loved the feel of her nuzzling back against his palm. "You were fun, brave, and adventurous. You were sexy, daring, and spoke your mind. You shimmered." He bent to kiss her. "All of those are qualities you haven't lost."

The tremulous smiles she returned made his heart ache. It was as if she had been starving for that reassurance. It pained him to see her everyday struggle with this confusing phase in her life. Then there was the lingering guilt; the knowledge that there was still more to their story, still more that he was holding back from her out of fear that she would hate him if she knew.

Instead, he shoved it all to the back of his mind and slowly began to lead her in a dance, even though there was no music. She seemed to hear what he was hearing and fell into step, resting her head on his shoulder and closing her eyes. Never had he wanted her more. Never had he wanted more urgently to meld his body to a woman's.

The time is now, he decided. Desire and lust and tenderness and love all fought for dominance in his body and heart. When she lifted her eyes to meet his, he knew that she was feeling the same.

Silently, so as not to break the spell, he took her by the hand and stepped back, searching her face. "You sure?" he asked.

She nodded mutely.

Hand in hand, they walked up the corridor to Seb's room, where they peeked in to admire the beautiful little person they had created together. Then, they went on to Justin's room, where the bed was bigger than hers, with so much more space for passionate play.

Upon entering the room, she stopped in the middle of the floor, immobile. He wanted to fall at her feet and worship, so he did.

Dropping to his knees, he wrapped his arms around her and pressed his face to her belly, inhaling her womanly scent, feeling it infuse every pore. His hands slid up under her dress, along the smooth skin of her legs and thighs, to cup and mold the roundness of her bottom. They were deliciously warm. So firm and inviting.

He grasped both cheeks and pulled Jalissa's hips forward, pressing his face against her mound, rubbing his cheek against the soft, warm fabric. Hooking his thumbs into the elastic waistband of her panties, he slowly pulled them down before allowing them to fall to the floor where he helped her step out of them.

It made him unbearably excited to know that she was otherwise fully dressed. It felt forbidden, naughty. Justin stroked and kneaded her bottom, scratching her skin lightly until she placed a hand in his hair for balance. He chuckled. "You know what's coming, don't you?"

She refused to rise to the bait, instead answering stubbornly, "N-no. Idea."

"Then let me refresh your memory." He lifted her skirt and slipped his head underneath to find neatly trimmed curls nestled between her legs. The sight and scent overpowered him, making him dizzy with the memories of the months with longing. After the year and a half of self-imposed celibacy he'd endured, all the while waiting and hoping that she would come back to him... his mouth was watering in anticipation.

"Justinnnn!" Jalissa groaned out his name impatiently, pressing on the back of his head impatiently.

The tip of his tongue snaked out, flicking at the folds of her skin, and he felt the immediate clenching of her buttocks under his hands. He was filled with malicious glee; the desire to torture her with tiny little flicks of the tongue when he knew she was hungering for more. And this he did, until her wetness pooled in his mouth, and he began to lap at her with greater intensity, his desire fueling her own.

"Don't... let me... fall." she gasped.

Justin lifted his mouth away just long enough to promise, "I will always catch you."

Jalissa gave in with a mighty shudder and a flood of warmth that he lapped up greedily. Getting back to his feet took more effort than he'd ever admit. He was so erect it was painful. With a deep kiss he shared with Jalissa the salty taste of her own moisture and was thrilled when she opened her mouth to accept it.

"We'd better lie down," he suggested, "Because it's beginning to look like *I'd* be the one to fall over."

"I will always catch you," she echoed with a smile, but allowed him to lead her to the bed.

Once there, he undressed her reverently, peeling away her dress and bra, marveling at her endless supply of beautiful, finely crafted underwear. *Not only did she taste good*, he thought, *she had good taste.* That made him chuckle.

"What?" she demanded.

Rather than answer, he stood and began stripping off his own clothes with greater haste and less care than he had hers. "Nothing."

"Are you laughing at me?" she asked in mock anger.

"Never, Sweetheart," he vowed as his body covered hers. Skin to skin, they stared into each other's eyes, exchanging warmth and emotion. He wished it would never end, but she was eager, pressing her body against his, widening her legs so that the tip of his penis naturally found itself pointing toward her opening. So, with gentle, probing thrusts, he made his way in, cognizant of the fact that it had been a long time for Jalissa and that her body needed to learn to accommodate him once more.

In a few moments, he was buried as deeply as her body would allow. Justin couldn't hold back the groan that passed his lips at the sheer pleasure of the moment. It was as if he'd found his way home.

The moment of reflection didn't last long as their carnal natures egged them on, demanding that they begin to move against each other. Justin began a pulsing tempo, angling his body so that he could see her expression as he did so, enjoying their connection.

With one hand, Jalissa caressed the nipple of her right breast. With the other she stroked his chest, fingers drifting through the lightly curled hairs.

The sensation of being inside of Jalissa after so long apart was overwhelming. When she lifted her toned legs and wrapped them around his back, his excitement rose, breaking what control he'd managed to maintain. Justin began to thrust more deeply into her, harder and faster, as if the blur of movement could obliterate all the differences between them; all the unresolved issues.

They were making love; connected, body and soul. It was sublimely dangerous, and dangerously sublime. Briefly, it passed through his mind that they both had so much to lose. But that treacherous thought was washed away by the intense pleasure that jolted down his spine, letting him know that his orgasm was fast approaching. Justin focused all of his energies upon Jalissa, making sure to take her with him. He took in the sight of her face as she screwed her eyes tight, gritted her teeth, face taut with her heated release, and only then did he let himself go.

Chapter 14

J alissa stretched luxuriously as she wandered out of Justin's room. It was the third straight morning that she'd woken up in Justin's bed, in his arms, and she was beginning to think that it would suit her just fine if she happened to do so every morning from now on.

The man's loving was exquisite; tender when she needed it, and rough and rugged when she was in that frame of mind, too. And after the loving was over and they lay in each other's arms in a sweaty heap, the next phase began, in which they snuggled, holding hands and gently whispering about inconsequential things.

Sheer heaven.

She stopped dead. Awful Nanny was standing at the entrance to the corridor that led to the bedrooms, and it was perfectly obvious that she knew what room Jalissa had just exited. It was also perfectly obvious that Nanny didn't approve. As a matter of fact, if it was humanly possible for a person to turn green, she would have.

I need to do something about her, Jalissa resolved. She understood that Justin had been the one to hire her, but surely she had a say in who took care of her baby? The level of tension in the house whenever Justin was gone was untenable. It was time to put a stop to this nonsense.

Since the other woman's arms were empty, Jalissa assumed that Sebastian was in the nursery. Sure enough, he was dozing in his crib. With a quiet huff, Jalissa took a moment to remove the fluffy woolen sweater that Seb was wearing. The nanny seemed to think he needed to wear warm clothes indoors. Who puts a baby to sleep in a sweater?

Looking around the room, Jalissa noticed a pile of plastic building blocks on the floor, next to a heap of documents and a set of blueprints, neatly bundled into scrolls. She smiled when she thought of father and son keeping each other company in the early morning, both doing their "job".

Once again looking at Seb, Jalissa realized that the stuffed iguana she'd bought him was missing. Considering that he'd taken to sleeping with it every night, it was strange that he wouldn't have it now. After a quick search, it was clear that it wasn't in the nursery, so Jalissa headed for the kitchen. Something was wrong here. Big stuffed toys didn't just disappear.

"Lorena?" she didn't even try to keep the sharpness out of her voice.

"Yes, Madame Jalissa?" The answer was as sweet as pie.

It was only then that she noticed two things: First was that the dress Lorena was wearing was more suited to a poolside party, rather than for taking care of someone's child. The material was far too thin for the season, and both the neckline and hem bared a generous helping of skin. Lorena's blonde hair was carefully combed into ringlets, as opposed to her normal, professional-looking bun.

Second, the table in the breakfast nook had been set for two and there were two used breakfast settings there. Jalissa knew that from time to time Lorena had shared a meal with Justin, but this had not been bacon and eggs. The pastry boxes on the counter were immediately recognizable as having come from her favorite pastry shop. A glass jug sat beside the empty plates, partly filled with juice. *Probably hand squeezed*, Jalissa grumbled internally.

Clearly, the woman had been making a move. A wave of territorial anger rolled through Jalissa. She would definitely address that later, but right now she had more important business to attend to. "Have you seen Cucumber?" she demanded.

Lorena looked profoundly innocent. "What?"

"My son's stuffed iguana," she responded curtly. Her patience with this woman was at an end. "Where is it?"

Lorena laughed a tinkling laugh. "Oh, that? I threw it out."

"*What?*" Jalissa couldn't believe what she was hearing.

"He spilled a cup of grape juice all over it. And you know how grape juice stains. Washing it would have been a nightmare, so I threw it out."

Lorena was still smiling cheerfully as she proceeded to prepare a plate of pastries and poured Jalissa a cup of orange juice, offering them up as if everything was settled. "Justin said to make sure you got breakfast. He went out early to get it just for you. He said these croissants are your favorite."

Jalissa glared from the plate to the woman and back again. "No, thank you. I'm not hungry." She was too furious about Cucumber to swallow a bite.

Lorena pulled her lips down dramatically. "Aww., are you sure? They're delicious. Justin and I enjoyed them so much!"

"I'm sure," Jalissa ground out.

Lorena shrugged and sighed gustily. "Fine." She set down the glass of juice on the table right in front of Jalissa and then dumped the plate of croissants into the sink. "At least drink the juice. Justin said he's been squeezing oranges for you every morning."

He had for the last few mornings. They'd even shared a glass of fresh juice in bed. Grudgingly, she took it up and brought it to her lips, inhaling the scent of fresh Naples oranges. Her favorite. Without another word, she spun on her heel and returned to her room. Jalissa'd had enough. She and Justin were going to have it out when he got home.

That woman had to go.

* * *

"Jalissa!" Justin's voice was frantic, etched with worry, and he was shaking her roughly by the shoulder.

Slowly Jalissa sat up, her head in a wreath of clouds. Why was she in her bed?

"Wake *up!*" he insisted.

She frowned. It wasn't like him to shout, especially not at her. She looked at the window and realized to her surprise that the sun was on the other side of the house. Half the day was gone.

"What?" she asked blearily.

"Where's Seb, Jalissa? Where's our son?"

Invoking that precious name was all it took to snap her out of her puzzled daze. "What do you mean?"

"What do I *mean?*" he roared. "What's going on? Where is our child?"

Jalissa threw her legs over the side of the bed and stood, only to discover to her horror that the carpet was soaked with chilly water. Cold fear began to grip her heart.

Instinct had her running for the nursery, with Justin keeping pace. With every step found herself in ankle deep in freezing cold water. Seb's nursery was a disaster. The water was deeper there, and everything floated: his toys, his books, even the business documents that Justin had forgotten on the floor this morning. Jalissa practically threw herself into the bathroom, choking on her fear. The bathtub was full to overflowing but, mercifully, there was no child in it.

"I turned it off," he snarled, "since you didn't seem to have the time to bother."

She was aghast at the accusation. "Do you think I that I left it on?"

"I don't have time for this discussion," he snapped. "We need to find Seb."

The next ten minutes were filled with sheer terror, as they raced from room to room, searching under beds, within closets, even out in the garden. By the time they returned to the house to repeat the same futile search, Jalissa was in tears.

"If something's happened to him–" Justin began. His face was a thunder-cloud, and his anger rolled toward her like black smoke, making her shudder.

Jalissa never found out what he was about to threaten, because the front door opened and in sailed Lorena with Sebastian in her arms, saying in a cheerful, sing-song voice, "We're baaack!"

Both parents rushed to the nanny's side, but it was Jalissa who snatched her son from Lorena's arms, clutching him against her breast, gasping with sobs of relief. Lorena proceeded toward the nursery, mouth agape. "What happened here? There's been a flood!" She turned to Jalissa. "Did you leave the bath on again?"

"What do you mean, 'again'?" Jalissa gasped.

Lorena looked at Justin regretfully. "I didn't want to say anything, because

I didn't want Jalissa to feel bad. But I caught it just in time once or twice."
Then she addressed Jalissa, her voice dripping honey. "I know it's hard for
you to stay focused sometimes, Dear, because of your... injuries."

The gall of this woman!

Justin looked from Lorena to Jalissa, frowning. "Why did you take Sebastian? Where did you take him?" he demanded.

Lorena looked at Jalissa, puzzled. "Jalissa asked me to take him to the park,
so she could get some rest—"

"I never!"

"Don't you remember?" Lorena placed a compassionate hand on Jalissa's
arm. "You said you couldn't manage him and all his antics today, and that
you needed a nap."

Realization struck. "Nap? You drugged me! You put something in that juice
you gave me!"

"What juice?" Lorena asked, her blue eyes as wide as they could possibly
go.

Never had Jalissa wanted to slap someone more. She wondered if Old Jalissa
was prone to brawling, among all her shortcomings, because if so she would
welcome the chance to flatten that treacherous bitch where she stood.

Lorena kept laying it on, thick as butter. "Are you sure you're feeling okay?
Is it your," she lowered her voice to a whisper, "head wound?"

"That's it! Enough." Jalissa turned to Justin, eyes pleading. "Justin, this
woman has been campaigning against me from the get-go. She has been
constantly trying to make me look crazy. Making it look like I would hurt
Sebastian. I would *never* hurt him!"

"That's insane," Lorena answered with deadly calm. "Why would I want to
hurt you? I love Seb like he's my own."

"*You're* insane!" Jalissa shot back. She turned to face Justin, pressing Seb
against her breast, who by now was aware of the tension in the room and was
squirming. "Justin, you can choose to believe me, or you can choose to believe
her. But you can't believe us both. What's it to be?"

He looked around himself, at the soaked carpet and his ruined business
documents, and then from Lorena's patently innocent face to Jalissa's agitated

one. He didn't have to think long. His eyes held Jalissa's for several seconds, and then he turned to Lorena and said, "Come with me."

* * *

Justin shut the door behind them and then faced Lorena squarely. With everything inside him, he struggled to remain in control of his anger. Could it be possible that this woman, who he had trusted with his child on a daily basis, had been plotting against Jalissa? But why?

Then Justin remembered Finn jokingly suggesting that the younger woman was sweet on him. Thinking back, Justin could recall the way he'd sometimes caught her looking at him, doe eyes fluttering. There was the occasional baring of a leg; the "forgotten" top button undone. Had he become so used to ignoring women who looked at him with desire or sought his attention that he failed to notice it happening on his own turf?

A cold mask replaced his normally warm countenance. Arms folded across his chest, shoulder squared, Justin looked at Lorena. Really looked at her.

"I am going to ask you one single question, and you have only one chance to answer," he informed her, all pleasantries gone. The easy, comfortable relationship he'd forged with her had evaporated. They were employer and employee. And this employee was in a heap of trouble. "Have you been deliberately trying to make it look like Jalissa is incapable of taking care of our son?"

Lorena took a step toward him. "Justin—"

"I asked you a question." His voice was low, frighteningly so. Remembering how he'd roared at Jalissa when he'd found Seb missing, Justin felt ashamed. But he knew that there was a stage of anger beyond yelling—and that was the white cloud of calm that was even now enveloping him. It was far more deadly than a yell.

Apparently, Lorena didn't realize the danger she was in and stepped forward again. Her lips curved into an odd little smile. "You don't understand. She doesn't belong here. She isn't good for Seb. I am. You and I are. All those months, we took care of him just fine. We don't need anyone else to help us raise him."

"First of all, there is no 'we'. Second, Jalissa is his mother."

The woman looked genuinely confused. "But I thought... you're always so nice to me. I figured I can be Sebastian's mother and you..." Lorena pursed her lips, her eyes hardening as if a decision had just been made. Then, to his horror, she began to unbutton the ridiculously low-cut blouse she was wearing.

"What the hell are you—"

Lorena grabbed his hand and rammed it against her breast, which was now heaving dramatically, as if she was having conniptions. "You know this is what you want. Not *her,*" she threw a sneering look in Jalissa's direction. "This." She pulled his hand closer.

Justin snatched his hand away as if it burned, then stalked behind his desk to put distance—and a huge piece of furniture—between them. The girl was clearly insane, and it sickened him to think that he had trusted her with his child. With a few quick moves, he wrote out a check, returned to face her, and shoved it at her. "Here is your payment for the month, plus severance. Your services are no longer required. You have three minutes to collect your things and then get out."

Lorena looked poleaxed, but to his relief, didn't cry or plead. He followed her to the kitchen to collect her things, return her keys, and then head to the door.

"How will I get into town?" she asked, suddenly docile and helpless.

"I don't care," he snapped, infuriated that she would dare try such as act on him after... "Call a cab. Walk if you like. Just. Get. Off. My. Property." He leaned closer to her face, to make sure she understood. "And if I ever see you anywhere near my family again, I promise you, you *will* regret it."

Showing that she had some self-preservation, Lorena hurried away, face pale and head lowered.

Justin hit the switch to open the gate and waited there until he was sure she was gone and his property secured. He then went in search of Jalissa to apologize, and promise to never doubt her capabilities again.

Chapter 15

Jalissa was surprised at how much she was enjoying the Mommy and Me group sessions at the community center. It was the kind of thing that seemed awfully silly until you had a child. At which point you craved the opportunity to share experiences with other moms, look for advice and support, all while your kids played in a safe, nurturing environment.

Eight or ten kids sipped on apple juice and clambered all over each other in a heap; looking like a litter of puppies. Meanwhile, the moms sat around and sipped tea and nibbled on the platter of lovely pastel-colored macarons Jalissa had brought to share.

"These are amazing!" said the woman on her left. She was a remarkably tall and capable-looking brunette called Melanie, who Jalissa had been on good terms with ever since they'd bonded over a disaster involving Sebastian, Melanie's twins, and a bottle of Elmer's glue one of the kids had swiped off a table.

Jalissa smiled gratefully. "Thank you. Seems like I can hardly tear myself away from the kitchen these days."

"Oh? You like baking?"

"I like it all, although I have to admit baking has its special appeal. It's so relaxing, you know?"

"I know what you mean. I learned to cook at my grandmother's elbow. I've loved it ever since!"

The memory of her own grandmother brought a smile to Jalissa's lips. "Me too! Cooking with your grandma, or even your mom, sets you up for a lifelong passion, doesn't it?"

Melanie finished one macaron and happily tucked into another. "It does. I even decided to make it my career. I opened up an intimate family dining restaurant four years ago. I figured I'd try to turn something I loved into a source of income, you know?"

"Sounds wonderful. How's it going?"

Melanie swallowed her bite of macaron and then stared down at the piece left in her hand, looking sad and contemplative. "Not so good these days. My cook got head-hunted by a restaurant in San Francisco. Upped sticks and left without so much as giving notice. And she'd been with me from the beginning!"

No cook? Jalissa felt bad for Melanie, but her heart leaped, nonetheless. What if...? Could she? Should she? "I can help you, if you want!" she blurted eagerly.

Melanie gave her a surprised look. "Help me? Are you sure?"

Now that the bee was in her bonnet, she refused to let it escape. "Yes! I'm an excellent cook! I even trained formally!" True, she still didn't remember taking the classes, but she had the certification to prove it, and she was sure that the knowledge was still buried in her head, just waiting to be accessed. Hadn't she been cooking for Justin almost all month?

"Give me a chance," she pleaded. "Let's set something up. A trial. I can come to your restaurant and prepare three courses. If you like it, you can take me on for a month."

She waited on Melanie's answer, hoping that her eagerness didn't show on her face. But inside, a voice was saying, *please-please-please.*

Melanie finished her macaron in a single bite, relishing it, and then handed over her business card with a smile. "Honey, if your main courses are anything like your macarons, I'll be lucky to have you."

The Mommy and Me session wrapped up, and Jalissa returned home with Seb, eager to share her news with Justin. In the days since that dreadful encounter with Lorena, he had been extra accommodating to her, as if he was deeply ashamed of not believing her, and wanted to make it up to her.

Justin had hired a large cleaning crew for the daunting cleanup operation, which included replacing the carpet and some furniture in Seb's room. It took a couple of days, thus sparing them the nightmare of prolonged disaster recovery, which meant they'd spent a week in the two-bedroom condo apartment Kalilah had leased when she'd first returned to Montreal for a divorce from Finn.

Of course, Jalissa had forgiven him and they'd sealed the deal during that first night in the condo with a long, slow, sweet session of lovemaking that had lasted well into the early hours. She had begun to crave his touch so intensely that when he left the house for work, she felt as if the very marrow in her bones was missing. One day while they both played with Seb on the floor of the condo, she'd asked him about how he'd spent the eighteen months she was in the coma.

"Just come right out and ask what you want to know," he said with a sigh.

He was right. They shared a bed, a baby and were engaged so she had a right to know if he slept with anyone while she was in the coma.

"Did you have sex with anyone while I was comatose? It was a long time to be celibate." She didn't know how she would feel if he said yes. On one hand she was close to death but on the other...

"Jalissa," he began, and before he could say anything else, Seb began to wail. Jalissa gathered her son in her arms and rocked him. When Seb finally fell asleep and Justin carried him to the crib in the spare bedroom Justin came up behind her in the kitchen and pinned her against the counter.

His masculine scent and power surrounded her like a warm blanket, causing goosebumps against her flesh. He nibbled on her ear and warmth pooled within her center.

"It's easy to be celibate when the one person you care for is fighting for her life. When that person is carrying your baby and the doctors aren't sure that either will survive, sex is the last thing on your mind. The only thing on your mind is their health and recovery." He paused to kiss down her neck, and she moaned. When he stopped the tingling trail and returned to her ear, she opened her mouth to protest, but he cut her off. "For nine months I prayed for the health of our baby and the strength of his mother to survive his birth.

I moved from Ottawa to Montreal and bought the house that, before your accident, you'd stare at while we drove and tell me it only needed some love and it would be perfect for a family. I spent more than ten hours a day renovating and reading building designs for our house. The other hours I spent at your bedside, talking to you and watching our growing son move within you. When the miracle of Seb's birth happened, I spent the next nine months caring for our son so that when you woke up, everything would be perfect for you."

He turned her around to face him now. His grey eyes were now glossy. "No, I didn't have time to have sex with anyone else. I was too busy planning our future, praying for your recovery, and pestering Kaiya and your doctors. I haven't looked at another woman since I saw you two years ago."

"Justin..." before Jalissa could finish what she was about to say, he claimed her full lips and lifted her unto the counter. What followed was wild, heated and intense.

The following days at the condo were spent playing with their son, barbecu- ing, cooking together and playing board games. At night, after putting their son to bed, they discussed varied topics like politics, climate change and even their relationship before her accident. Justin only answered what she asked concerning their relationship and added in nothing more, which made her wonder about their past relationship. Jalissa learned more about the man she was engaged to like the fact that he had wanted a daughter instead of a son and he was more of a pig person verses having a cat or a dog. She also learned that the condo where they were currently staying might have been where their son was conceived.

They were in a good place now, and she'd do anything not to disrupt that.

When they finally returned home, it was almost as if nothing had ever happened.

Even though the past week felt like it had been heaven, Jalissa knew it was time for the next step. Somehow she needed to find a way to make use of her talents, especially after having been cooped up for so long.

As soon as they got home, Jalissa burst into Justin's home office with Seb in her arms, crackling with electric excitement. "Justin!" She realized he was on the phone and had to cool her heels in anguish for another two minutes before he concluded his business and hung up.

He gave her an indulgent, welcoming smile. "That must have been some Mommy and Me class."

"You haven't heard the half of it!" Jalissa proceeded to spill out all the details, about how well she and Melanie had been getting along, about the problems at the restaurant, and how excited she was at the possibility of working there. "I could be getting a job, Justin. A real job!"

His face was impassive, and she wasn't sure that was altogether a good thing.

"Do you *want* a job?" he finally asked her.

"Yes, of course. What do you—"

"We have more than enough money for you to stay home and care for our son for as long as you want."

She knew that, but this was different. Why didn't he understand? "Yes," she acknowledged. "And I'm not ungrateful. But this is my chance to do something for me, while also helping others. I'm a good cook. I know I can do this."

Pushing back his chair, Justin rose and walked around the desk to stand in front of her. He took her free hand in both of his and smiled down at her. "Being a chef in a restaurant is a lot more work than just making dinner for us here at home," he reminded her. "You'll be on your feet for hours. Are you sure you're physically able to take on the task?"

Not this again! "A couple of weeks ago you promised to believe that I am capable. I'm not handicapped. I can do this," she reminded him.

Justin examined her face for what felt like forever to Jalissa, and then his own softened. "Very well. I believe in you. Set up an appointment, and I'll be there. Okay, sweetheart?"

She couldn't have been happier.

* * *

Justin held Jalissa's hand as they walked into the restaurant, while Seb, held in the other arm, settled comfortably against his shoulder. All the way downtown he'd listened indulgently as Jalissa chatted excitedly about her trial menu, which would be simple and quick, with fresh ingredients and a flavorful selection of spices.

It made him happy to see her so fired up and confident. Although he was capable of caring of Jalissa and Seb financially as long as they needed him to, he understood how much it meant to her to have some independence, as well as a creative outlet for her talents.

He just wished she'd take it slowly. After all, it wasn't long ago that she had been flat on her back in a hospital bed, unmoving and insensible. Was her body up to the physical demands she would be placing upon it?

But Jalissa was Jalissa - fiery, determined, and strong - and that was just the way he loved her. Why would he think she would be—or should be—willing to compromise?

The owner was waiting eagerly at the door to greet them and, after introductions, she invited them inside. Justin drew back during the short tour; it was Jalissa's day, not his. The restaurant, simply called *Melanie's*, was warm and cozy, beautifully lit and nicely furnished, and with his trained eye Justin could tell that it had a lot of potential to do well.

As they entered the kitchen, the women chattered excitedly and Justin faded comfortably into the background. He found a seat in one corner with Seb on his lap, sucking happily on a chocolate wafer that Melanie had offered him. He watched with great admiration as Jalissa whirled around the kitchen like a dervish, chopping, sautéing, sprinkling and tasting. When she was done—in record time—they sat together to enjoy the meal.

"Darling!" Melanie enthused, "This calamari! How did you do it?"

"Grandma's recipe," she answered, and winked at Justin.

Melanie lifted her glass. "Here's to grandmas everywhere. When can you start?"

The women began negotiating, and from time to time Justin stepped in to ask for clarifications or offer suggestions, using his own knowledge of the business to ensure that Jalissa got the best possible terms. Despite his interference, Melanie didn't seem the least bit perturbed, bowing instead to the knowledge of someone who was well known in the restaurant industry. Whose name meant something.

When negotiations were over, the women stood, hugged, and kissed each other on both cheeks. "I'll have your documents ready for you to sign when you come in tomorrow," Melanie promised.

Jalissa clapped her hands together in a surprisingly girlish gesture. "I'm so excited! I can't wait!" She threw Justin a glowing glance that made him melt, then hugged Melanie again. "Thank you!"

"Thank *you*," Melanie countered, and saw them to the door. "Pleasure to meet you, Justin."

"Same here. And take care of my Jalissa, will you?"

Melanie glanced from one to the other, beaming. "Oh, I will!"

He took Jalissa's hand again, relishing the feel of it, glad that she wasn't pulling away. They were acting like a family more and more, and he didn't want that to end. "What do you say we take Seb for some ice cream? He just whispered that he's craving a big scoop of strawberry."

She twinkled at him, still riding on a high of pure joy. "Oh, Seb told you that, did he?"

"Yes, Mademoiselle, he did."

"Then let's not disappoint him."

Hours later, when Seb had had his sugar crash and was fast asleep in his crib, the pair had fallen into their own bed. Justin held Jalissa in his arms, enjoying the feel of her braids splayed across his chest. Her fine motor skills were so good now that she was able to nimbly and swiftly do her hair in any style she pleased, but he'd always liked her braids best, the way they framed her face and accentuated her strong, determined look.

They'd been kissing and caressing each other for what felt like hours, coming together and then dancing away to prolong the excitement. Putting off that moment when he claimed her body elicited every ounce of pleasure within her.

In an idle fashion, Justin toyed with her hands, stroking the length of her fingers. She and Kaiya had popped out to the spa just the day before and her manicure, though short and neat as befitted a chef, was also pretty, sparkly and feminine. Remarkably, the vibrant red was close to the color of the Kawasaki motorbike that still stood in his garage, waiting for its owner.

Staring down at their clasped hands, Jalissa asked, completely out of the blue, "Where's my ring?"

"Hmm?"

"My engagement ring. Did you keep it?"

The question blindsided him, leaving him momentarily speechless. God. A ring. How stupid could he be? How could he have forgotten? With her eyes were on his, curious and waiting, he had to answer fast.

He swallowed. "Actually, there isn't a ring."

Her beautifully shaped brows shot up. "We were engaged, and I didn't have a ring?"

"We didn't have time to get one. I proposed only days before your accident. Just days before you found out about—"

"My pregnancy."

"Yes," he hurried on, not wanting to linger on that point, lest everything else fall apart. "You'd said yes, but we agreed that we'd go shopping over the weekend for a ring, so you could pick out what you wanted."

"Oh," Jalissa breathed out. "I guess that makes—"

Stop, he thought. *I need to stop this right now, before this conversation goes down a rabbit hole we can't escape from.* Justin drew her close, planting a kiss on her lips. It had the desired effect. The ring was forgotten and Jalissa pressed back against him, opening her mouth softly under his.

The excitement of the day translated into increased desire; he could feel it flow through her body like a high-pitched vibration. Her hands slid under his shirt, seeking his nipples through the crisp hair on his chest, finding them already tight. Brushing against them with her thumbs, drawing a groan from him.

"I love how broad and strong your chest feels," Jalissa murmured as she helped him remove the shirt.

"You make me feel strong," he replied. "No. Wait... When you touch me like that, you make me feel weak."

The smile she flashed at him made his heart, and other parts of him, swell. Then she pressed her lips against the closest of his nipples, sucking on it gently, then with increasing cruelty; causing him to harden further down below. He felt her short, sharp nails scratch lightly against his straining biceps. This was a woman who wasn't afraid to give as good as she got during sex. He loved that about her.

Justin wanted her so badly. The smart business dress, which he had so admired when she'd dressed to go to the restaurant, had become nothing more than an annoying barrier between him and what he needed. He tugged impatiently at it until Jalissa laughed and removed his hands from the unwilling buttons.

"If you pop one of my buttons, I'm going to have to punish you," she joked.

Punish him...? Not a bad idea. He watched with hungry eyes as she peeled off her dress and wriggled out of her bra and panties. Then she lay back on the bed, the cream sheets contrasting sharply with the warm glow of her dark skin.

Starting at the crown of her head and moving downward, he pressed gentle kisses, deliberately avoiding her lips even though she struggled to capture his. Down past her jaw and delicate throat, down her shoulders and missing her breasts completely, which caused her to howl in frustration. "Justin!"

When he arrived at her belly, Justin lingered, slipping his tongue into the hollow of her navel, then traveling a few inches lower to that barely visible scar. The place where they had cut into her flesh to extract their precious little boy. He kissed it reverently.

Justin noted that her pelvic bones, which had been so stark and sharp after she'd left the hospital, were now nicely cushioned as she'd begun to fill out again and regain her former, glorious curves. As he pressed his face against her left hip, his hands slid around to grasp her firm, but equally resilient, cheeks; enjoying their smooth roundness.

Jalissa's hips arched, and she pressed her mound toward his lips in an unspoken plea, but he chose instead to prolong her agony. Forgoing that valley of delight, he moved even lower, kissing her thighs, leaving a trail along her legs, until he arrived at her beautifully pedicured feet. As with her fingers, the polish on her toenails was a brilliant red.

Each toe received a kiss before he sucked the littlest one on her left foot into his mouth. Jalissa bucked like a marlin on a hook. *Enough,* he thought. He was done torturing them both. It was time to bring her true pleasure.

Justin shifted his body so that the light puff of soft curls was directly before him. They were beaded with a fine dew of moisture, proof of how aroused she was, and how much she wanted him.

Gently, with both thumbs, he parted those lips, feasting his eyes on the dark folds within; imagining them to be some exotic, fragrant orchid. Flicking at her with just the tip of his tongue, he rejoiced in the way she writhed and the noises she made. Without warning, he increased the pressure; soaking up the heat and moisture. Justin loved the way she tasted. He wished he could feast on her like this every day until the day he died.

Instead of feeling her hands pressing his head closer as he'd come to expect, she grasped him by the hair and tried to drag him up to face her. "I need you inside me. Now. Justin, please!"

He complied without complaint, positioning himself between her legs and pressing the tip of his erection against her willing opening. A single swift movement sent him plunging into her with enough force to rock her back against the mattress.

Now, they were locked in a dance choreographed by nature; moving against each other, in a tempo that grew faster and faster until there was nothing left in the universe except the two of them and their need for each other.

When they finally collapsed into each other's arms, both of them had forgotten about the ring.

Chapter 16

They say that if you can't stand the heat you need to get out of the kitchen, but Jalissa thrived in the heat. It made her feel energized, creative... Alive. It was her first night at *Melanie's* and she was in the kitchen yelling instructions at her new crew. She was one staff member short tonight. Not a great place to start, but she was determined not to let it slow her down. All she needed to do was work both faster and smarter. Right?

Melanie herself had no problem buckling down and chipping in behind the line to help pick up the slack, but most of the time she was out front, welcoming her guests. Many of whom had heard she had a new chef and had come in to satisfy their curiosity as to whether she was a keeper.

No pressure, right?

Jalissa sped from station to station, smelling and tasting. The salmon mousse was flawless, but the mussels needed more white wine. When she discovered that an entire wheel of Roquefort was spoiled, she wanted to cry. Dish after dish went speedily out to the service area, but as fast as she covered the orders, more came in.

She stopped, just for a second, to catch her breath. Was she up to the task, she wondered? Was she able to do this, or had she stepped out of her comfort zone too soon? Maybe–

No. Giving up now would be unthinkable. That wasn't who she was. She'd fought her way through a coma, dammit. She could ace this!

But then...

"Jalissa!" Melanie's breathless voice broke into her thoughts.

Jalissa startled guiltily. Did Melanie think she'd been slacking off on the job?

But Melanie was smiling broadly. "You have visitors." She gestured out through the kitchen doors.

Visitors? I don't have time for visitors! "But—"

Melanie shooed her outside. "Go on. I'll cover for you."

Dusting her hands on the front of her apron, Jalissa hustled outside to be greeted by the cheers of her friends. Justin, Kaiya, Tyler, Finn, and Kalilah, all seated around a large table, clapping as she approached them. "We're so proud of you!" Kaiya squealed, while Justin stood up and stepped around the table to press a kiss upon her forehead.

"Yes," he agreed. "We really are. We think you're amazing."

Jalissa pressed her hands against her mouth to keep herself from crying. She could say little more than, "Thank you, thank you." before hurrying back inside. Now, she wasn't just cooking to prove herself to a restaurant full of strangers, she was cooking to prove to a group of people who cared for her and believed in her that their trust was justified.

That knowledge gave her wings. And that night, her cooking brought the house down at *Melanie's*.

* * *

The wine was flowing and the mood around the table was light. Everyone oohed and aahed over Kalilah in her newly acquired maternity wear, since her baby bump was finally beginning to show.

Justin set down his knife and fork, replete from the delicious meal Jalissa had prepared, wondering how he was going to be able to fit in dessert. Knowing that Jalissa had prepared it, he decided he'd eat it all, even if it meant he'd split his sides doing so. She was an amazing cook, and he was grateful to have her in his life. And not just for her cooking.

"Damn, Justin," his brother said as he, too, finished the last bite and washed it down with one of the finest wines *Melanie's* had to offer. "Do you eat like this every night?"

Justin scoffed, "Actually, I do, but you're acting as if I can't handle my own in the kitchen. What did you think I did before Jalissa came along? Survived on cornflakes?"

"Okay, I'll give you that." Finn grinned at him. "You know as well as I do that being in the restaurant business teaches you a special skill in the kitchen. But sometimes, as they say, the shoemaker's children have no shoes."

"Our shoes are just fine," he joked back, motioning to his fully belly as proof.

Finn patted his lips with a linen napkin and laid it carefully next to his plate. "Speaking of restaurants. Can we have a word?"

Justin stood immediately, worry creasing his face. Was something going on with the family chain of restaurants? He was still rattled by the fire in the kitchen back in Ottawa.

"Ladies, Ty, excuse my brother and me a few moments, will you?"

"Family secrets?" Kalilah teased him.

"Something like that." Finn blew her a kiss, then led Justin out to the foyer.

"What's happening?" Justin asked, concerned.

"Don't worry. Nothing disastrous. I was just talking to Dad, and since they confirmed arson, they've deepened the investigation. We were thinking of increasing security at the other restaurants, just in case someone has a vendetta against our family."

All told, the Tremblay family owned ten fine dining restaurants and five fast service outlets. So, the possibility that they would be targeted for that kind of attack was disconcerting.

But aside from all of that, it stung just a little that their father had reached out to Finn, even though he had no participation in their family restaurant business. Since Justin was the one who'd flown all the way to Ottawa when the fire had happened, why didn't Dad call him first?

Finn must have known him very well, because he answered Justin's unspoken question. "He didn't want to call you, Justin, because he knows you have your hands full with Jalissa's recovery and taking care of Seb. It's not that he wanted my advice over yours."

That was news to him. "It's no big deal. You and dad are closer than he and I are," he confessed. Maybe it was the intimate family setting, and the good wine that had loosened his tongue. But he knew his brother well enough, and trusted him well enough, to feel that he was finally able to say something.

Finn dropped his jovial demeanor and took a step closer, resting an arm on Justin's. "I know it looks like Dad turns to me first, and I know he was grooming me to take over the business, but that's just because he thinks, as a man of honor, that the business should go to the elder. It's not because he trusts you less. Dad loves and trusts us both equally—"

"I know," he said thickly. "I just always felt I needed to prove myself to him."

"I think you have. You're successful. You're happy. You have a beautiful, talented fiancée and a wonderful son. And, more and more, you've become their rock." Finn paused, as if deep in thought, and then said, "You probably don't feel this way, but you were always the lucky one. Dad came into my life after years of my wondering where my dad was. And when he married Mom, I finally did. But you... you, Justin, were blessed. You've always had a father. You never had to suffer through those empty years like I did."

The emotion was thick - maybe a bit too thick - and all the two men could do was embrace each other awkwardly, then return to the table, smiling. As they lingered for another half hour or so, exclaiming in delight over the platter of brandy-infused profiteroles that Jalissa sent out to them, Justin felt lighter than he had in a long time. He loved his brother deeply, but there had always been this underlying sense of competition for their father's love and respect. Finding out that Finn had also gone through his own doubts and uncertainties as he was growing up made him feel a bit more secure that the playing field was level.

In time, the other two couples said their goodbyes. Seb was spending the night at Kaiya's, with TJ as a playmate and an excellent babysitter, so there was no urgency to go home. "I'll just wait on the chef," he said to the others. "Maybe she'll need a lift home."

"Maybe she'll reward you with a cookie," Kaiya joked, giving him a tight hug.

"I certainly hope so," he answered fervently.

The crowd of diners finally thinned out, as workers briskly began to clear up. Now that the music was off, and in the absence of chatter, he could hear the clatter in the kitchen and knew they were busy cleaning up and putting everything away for tomorrow.

Jalissa emerged, flushed, hot, and happy. As she removed her toque, her braids spilled out, framing her gorgeous face. He grabbed her up and spun her around. "You were amazing!"

"You think so?"

"Of course. If I'm not careful, you'll put a belly on me."

She patted him lightly on his granite abs. "I hope not!"

They walked companionably outside, into a surprisingly warm evening, heading toward the car. As he held the door open for her to slide inside, he couldn't resist adding, "You know I'm mad at you, right?"

Her face turned to his, as if she was half wondering if he was serious. "Why?"

"I'm still not sure how I feel about you doing such a good job working for the competition!"

Jalissa laughed out loud at the absurdity of that idea. "Oh, I'm sure of your family restaurants will survive the threat of little old me." She threw him a sly sidelong look. "Plus, I didn't want anyone to say I was sleeping with the boss to get want I want."

"That's where you're wrong," he leered at her like a wolf. "Sleeping with the boss will get you everywhere!"

They chuckled, holding hands as he sped off, taking the scenic route off the main highway, past a wide expanse of lake that glittered with the reflections of the skyscrapers and highway lights on the far side.

"Beautiful," she breathed, staring out the window.

"Want to stop?"

"What?"

Without waiting for an answer, Justin spun the wheel until the SUV rumbled off the paved road and onto the grassy shoulder, mere meters from the pebbly beach. "This is as good a place as any for what I have in mind," he announced.

"What do you have in mind?"

"This." He reached into his breast pocket and withdrew a long, slender jewelry box, offering it to her. "This is just a small token to let you know how

116

proud I am of how far you've come."

Eyes bright, she opened the box to reveal a slender white gold tennis bracelet, studded with red jasper. Her favorite color. "Oh, thank you."

Just the idea that he'd put that smile on her face made him warm all over. She proffered her slender wrist for him to clasp it on for her, but instead, he popped the box into the glove compartment. "Not yet," he said. "I have another idea."

Disappointment gave way to a puzzled look. "You have?"

He pointed at the silent, glittering lake with his chin. "It's a warm night..."

"Warm-*ish*," she corrected, looking out onto the water.

He ignored her half-hearted protest. "When last did you go skinny dipping?"

She gave a shocked squeal. "Are you mad?"

"Mad to see you buck naked and soaked to the skin," he countered.

"But people will see us!" She sounded scandalized, not a frequent occurrence with the Jalissa he used to know.

"Not if we're submerged. What goes on under the water, stays under the water." To preclude any argument, he began peeling off his shirt and wriggled out of his tailored trousers. "You aren't undressing," he pointed out. "What's the matter? Are you chicken?"

As he predicted, she rose to the bait. "Me? Chicken? Like hell."

By the time he was out of the car, she was standing on the grass, naked and splendid, looking so delectable that he nearly changed his mind and dragged her caveman-style back into the car. But before he could make good on his plans, she was off and running, her sleek skin glowing in the faint moon light

They hit the water's edge together, screaming in unison as the cold water closed around them. The night might have been warm, but the water certainly wasn't.

"We'll freeze!" she gasped, teeth already chattering.

"Come over here, let me warm you up."

"Only because you're warm," she insisted, slipping into his arms and allowing him to wrap her into a bear hug. "Not because you're cute or anything."

He was about to respond with a zinger, but the feel of her in his arms brought other thoughts into his head entirely. Even as the cool water lapped against his body, he became immediately erect. Then she wriggled against his bare skin, as supple and smooth as a dolphin. What probably began as an unconscious gesture swiftly turned into something wickedly deliberate, as Jalissa pressed her bare bottom against his erection, laughing as she did so. "Payback's a bitch," she reminded him.

"You think that's payback?" he asked through gritted teeth. "*This* is payback." With one hand, he steadied her, and with the other, he felt his way between her legs, finding his target, which was much warmer than the surrounding waters, and already slippery.

As he pressed against her entrance, she gasped, "We can't!"

"We can," he replied, and slid inside.

The combined effect of the chilly water, the wind that was whipping up, and the sheer naughtiness of making love outdoors, stark naked, to the sound of traffic whooshing by, heightened their excitement. They both knew this was no time for dawdling, no time to relish the sensation. They moved as one, building in speed and intensity, until moments later, they rode a wave of joy and sensation, and Jalissa fell back against his chest, limp and panting.

"That was—"

The yellow glare of headlights slashed across their bodies as a massive semi-truck passed by, the gleeful driver yanking on his horn in a congratulatory *toot-toot*.

Jalissa covered her face with an embarrassed squeal. "We're going to get arrested!"

He swept her up in his arms and ran with her back to the car. "Not if we aren't here!"

They fell inside, laughing like naughty schoolchildren. They knew that when they got home, they would have all the time they needed to take it slow.

Chapter 17

J alissa fell into a comfortable, happy routine: working at *Melanie's* three nights a week, and spending the rest of her time at home, building her bond with Sebastian and Justin.

They hired a new nanny who had been meticulously sourced and recommended by Kalilah. This time, they were relieved to find that she was a sane West Indian expat called Gwendolyn, who had raised five children and eight grandchildren. She informed them up front that nothing made her happier than making sure that "God's precious little ones" were happy, well fed and well taken care of.

Even so, Jalissa did everything she could to spend more time with Sebastian. Letting him sit in his highchair or bouncy swing while she worked in the kitchen, trying out new recipes to later replicate at the restaurant. She was happy that Justin was a willing guinea pig, who celebrated her culinary victories and gave her workable suggestions when her experiments were met with failure.

Something had shifted between them. There was a new sense of warmth and comfort whenever she and Justin were together. They made love frequently and, although she still maintained the guest bedroom as her own, more often than not she woke up in his bed, and in his arms.

Why then, she wondered, had they never reprised their conversation about their engagement and the ring he'd promised to buy her? Was Justin having doubts? For her, it was a lot to take in as her new life had only taken shape mere months ago. Jalissa was experiencing doubts herself, but things were good. Weren't they? She was growing increasingly aware of a feeling inside, which deepened every day, which took up more and more space inside her. Did she dare put a name to it?

"Cake time!" Kalilah announced cheerily. Friends and family were gathered in the spacious dining room: Finn and their kids, Kaiya, Ty, and TJ; Melanie and her twins; and a couple of Sebastian's other little friends from the Mommy and Me playgroup. The room was a kaleidoscope of bright colors, HAPPY BIRTHDAY banners and streamers, helium-filled balloons kissing the ceiling, heaps of shredded gift wrapping ankle-deep on the floor.

One year ago, even as she lay unconscious, her beautiful little boy had entered the world. It was such a miracle that sometimes she was struck silent with awe.

They sang Happy Birthday and, when Seb made it clear he had absolutely no idea that he was meant to blow out the single candle on top of the much-too-large unicorn-shaped cake that Melanie had brought them, Justin manfully did his duty. Soon, everyone was enjoying the pastel-marbled masterpiece with their choice of ice cream.

Around seven in the evening, Sebastian conked out while sitting on the floor surrounded by toy trucks and cars, stuffed toys and bouncy balls. He literally fell forward on his face, making them all laugh. "I guess that's our signal to say goodnight," Kaiya said. The guests began tidying up, but Jalissa insisted that they leave the mess. Tomorrow was another day, and the clutter would still be there. So, they hugged and kissed, wishing Seb all the blessings in the world as they filed out into the driveway.

Alone once again, Justin locked the front door as Jalissa gathered up her little bundle. "Let me just put him to bed," she offered. "Then I'll come outside and we can—"

But her little bundle was stirring, hopped up as he was on a heady combination of excitement and sugar, and was alert and laughing in her arms again. She gasped. "I can't believe it!"

"Believe it," Justin replied. "We Tremblay men don't ever quit!"

"You sure don't," was her saucy reply. She set Seb down on the floor and squatted beside him as Justin followed suit. Sebastian's bright eyes swept the room, overwhelmed by the abundance of his choice of toys, until he finally settled on a large green iguana. Jalissa's replacement for poor Cucumber, which Mean Nanny had thrown away.

"Is that the one you want? Do you want Zucchini?" Justin asked. He was about to reach for it and then froze. Sebastian had other ideas. Pushing up with his hands, the newly one-year-old boy got wobbly to his feet, wavered until he found his balance, then toddled over to Zucchini, before tumbling over onto the heap of soft green plush.

Jalissa and Justin shared a startled, delighted look. "Did you see that?"

"I did!" His face was the picture of glee. "Our baby's a toddler now!"

Our baby. The idea of it was so awe-inspiring that it stole Jalissa's breath. To think that she and Justin could have come together to create this miracle, to be able to create this tiny, perfect family, was more than she could imagine.

She scooted over to Justin, much as Sebastian was used to doing, and threw her arms around his neck. "This is perfect. This is a perfect night. I loved every minute of it—and I love you, Justin!"

When they both realized what she had said, they stared at each other, frozen as silence echoed throughout the room.

* * *

Justin didn't know what to think; how to feel. Jalissa had said those words: *I love you.* Words he had never heard falling from her lips or, at least, not directed toward him. The idea of it filled him with two conflicting emotions - joy and fear.

He had no doubt that she meant what she said - the woman didn't have a deceitful bone in her body - and the idea of being loved like this blew him away. He was silent for so long that a flush rose on her face. She put her hands to her lips as if hoping she could reclaim those words. But he didn't want her to. He didn't want to see her eyes filled with pain and embarrassment.

"I... are you okay?" she asked hesitantly.

"I'm great. It's just... this is amazing. I didn't expect–" What was wrong with him? Being lost for words wasn't a predicament he often found himself in. He knew that he felt deeply for her; always had. He knew he wanted her, desired her, wanted to be with her. But the knowledge of his past deceptions scared him. This fragile love of hers. Would it last if she knew what he'd done? The lies he'd told, even if he thought they were for the greater good?

They both rose to their feet in silent agreement, while Seb snuggled down on top of his plushy and dozed happily off again. Facing each other, searching each other's eyes. His brave Jalissa placed her hand on his and asked him again. "Are you okay, Justin?"

"I am." His voice sounded more confident, and he was glad for that. "I just wondered, are you sure? How you feel?"

Her lips curved up. "Of course, I am. I know I am. This is the happiest I've been. You, me, Seb." She waved her arm around the room. "All of this. It's so perfect. *We're* perfect. I can't imagine a life without the two of you. I can't imagine a home without the two of you. I love you, and I want us to be together."

It's time, he thought. Time to be courageous, step up, and be honest with her. It was the only way they would truly ever be happy. He wrapped his arms around her and pulled her close. "I love you too, Jalissa. You and Seb changed my life. And like you, I think that what we have now is perfect. But—"

The delight on her face dimmed a little at that final word. "But?"

"But there's something I need to tell you. There's stuff you need to know—"

Before he could draw another breath, Jalissa reached up on tiptoe and cut him off with a soft kiss. "Don't. You don't need to say anything more." To his shock, she dropped down to one knee. "Justin Tremblay, will you marry me?"

A surprised laugh erupted from his lips. Always going against the trend. How like this wonderful woman to do something that totally awed him. Justin hauled her back to her feet and held her in an even tighter embrace, lest she take it into her head to do anything sillier.

"I will," he said, and claimed her lips in a long, satisfying kiss, one that had his body stirring. Justin could feel her own body leaning into his in response and immediately thought of whisking her away to his room, but struggled against the urge. He had to be sure.

"Don't you want to wait until more of your memory comes back? So, you can be certain about what you're doing?"

Jalissa's braids bounced as she shook her head emphatically. "Nope. Why would I? I'm safe and happy and loved. Plus, it's been three months and I barely remember anything new. What if my memory never comes back? Would I have to wait forever for us to be a family?"

Justin nodded slowly. "What you're saying makes sense—"

"It does! Remembering my past life couldn't possibly change how I feel about you or Seb or everything we've built. And we were already engaged before my accident. So, we knew from the start that we wanted this. So please, Justin, let's just do this."

Giving in to what they both wanted, he grasped her left hand and planted a kiss on the finger where an engagement ring, and eventually his wedding ring, would sit. "Yes, my love. Let's just do this."

They held on to each other for a long time, but even that couldn't chase away the last cobwebs of guilt from Justin's mind.

* * *

Jalissa threw one final glance at the tea setting for two on the low table in Justin's sun room before opening the door to Kaiya. The two friends hugged each other, then they walked further into the room and Kaiya set TJ down before Sebastian. Those two also hugged, chattering away in a language that only toddlers understand.

"Ooh," Kaiya exclaimed as she sat. The table was laid with Justin's best china tea service, and an array of dainty dishes that Jalissa had spent the morning making, despite the fact that it was her day off and she should, theoretically, not want to set foot in a kitchen. There were tiny open-faced baby shrimp sandwiches, handmade oatcakes with a cream cheese and sundried tomato spread, and avocado slices on wholegrain toast. On the sweeter side, Jalissa had served strawberry scones with clotted cream, madeleines sprinkled with citrus zest, and butterscotch éclairs.

"You're a dangerous woman to know, Jalissa," Kaiya announced as she began placing delicacies on her plate. "By the time I walk out of here, I'll weigh a million pounds."

Jalissa poured the mint tea and poo-poohed the mere idea. "No, you won't. You have the metabolism of a dragonfly."

Kaiya bit into an éclair, closed her eyes in pleasure, then responded. "Maybe normally, but pregnancy is a whole 'nother ball game."

"What?" Jalissa squealed, her hands shaking with excitement, so much so that amber tea spilled from her cup into its saucer. "You're pregnant?"

"Yes, Ma'am." Kaiya grinned, radiating glee.

"What? When? How?"

Kaiya winked. "You know how."

Jalissa playfully swatted her friend on the arm. "You know what I mean. Did you guys plan this? Are you excited?"

"Yes, we did, and I am so excited. Ty is, too."

"I am so happy for you," she said sincerely. Jalissa waited until she'd put away a whole scone before saying, "Not to steal your thunder, but—"

Kaiya immediately looked down at Jalissa's flat belly. "Are you?"

Slapping her hands to her abdomen defensively, Jalissa exclaimed. "Me? No!" At least, she thought not. She and Justin hadn't been very careful, and you never knew how the universe worked. "What I mean is, we're getting married!"

"The engagement is back on the table? I was wondering what was happening with that. Did he propose to you again?"

"I proposed," she admitted with a sheepish grin. "But he said yes."

Kaiya hugged her. "I'm so happy. Do you love him?"

"I do. And he loves me, too."

"That's amazing. That's great. Especially since you don't remember the first time."

There was a thick silence that followed, one that Jalissa didn't like at all. "Kaiya? Is there something you want to tell me? Do you not think marrying Justin is a good idea?"

Kaiya gave her a stoic smile. "Of course, I think it's a good idea. It's just that I'm surprised. Just before you started seeing Justin, I remember you talked about tying your tubes."

Given how happy she was now, as a mother, the idea that she'd have considered such a permanent solution left her aghast. "What! That's drastic!"

"I know. You just swore you'd never have any children."

"Why? Why would I say that?"

Kaiya shrugged. "You never told me. But I never forgot what you said. Matter of fact..." She glanced uncomfortably in the direction of the nursery, where the laughter of the children could be heard. "Matter of fact," she pressed on, "Justin and I had a few arguments when you were in your coma, when we first discovered you were pregnant. I reminded him that you were against being a mother, but since he was your fiancé and presumably the baby's father, I allowed him to convince me of your carrying Seb to term."

After the argument he said they'd had and the awful things she'd told him, Justin had fought for her to have their baby? Even after she'd threatened to terminate? The idea that she might have had her way, and that Seb might not have been brought into existence, nauseated her, made her weak.

Suddenly not hungry anymore, she pushed her tea plate away and towards the empty area of the table. Kaiya did likewise. "The woman I was," she began tentatively, "wasn't such a nice person, was she?" She felt deeply ashamed, anguished.

Kaiya wasn't having it. "You had your quirks, sure. But then, we all do. All you need to know is that the woman you were was fierce and loyal, a talented, confident woman, and a great friend. And you are all those things today. That will never change."

Jalissa nodded slowly, grateful for Kaiya's reassurance. But throughout the rest of the afternoon, even when the conversation turned to lighter topics, she couldn't stop wondering. Did she really want all of her memories back? Did she really want to meet Old Jalissa face to face?

* * *

It seemed as though everything Justin and his family did, there was always food involved, Justin thought. It was food that brought their family together and, even when something else did, they celebrated the moment with food. From his office, he could hear the clatter of Jalissa, his mom and Violet in the kitchen, making dinner. Justin winced at the idea of what would happen when three great cooks got together and began arguing about who prepared what and how.

"Better in here than out there, huh, son?" his father joked, face crinkled with laughter at his own little joke.

Looking over at where his father sat, cradling Seb in his arms, Justin grinned. "You can say that again!"

His father had just been telling him the good news. The person behind the fire set in the Ottawa restaurant had been caught. An ex-employee of theirs, a sommelier who Justin's father had fired for repeatedly sexually harassing other staff members. Without a reference, the man had been unable to find a job and had decided the Tremblay family was responsible for his predicament. The kitchen fire had been his way of getting even. Now, he was looking at jail time.

"I'm so relieved to know it's all over," Justin admitted. "It was really weighing on my conscience."

"On your *conscience?*" his dad asked, puzzled. "Why?"

"Since you're semi-retired, it effectively happened under my watch. I'm the one responsible."

His father tried to placate him. "You were two hundred kilometers away."

Justin waved his hand. "Exactly. The buck stops with me. Even though," he paused. Did he really want to bring up anything so painful?

"Even though what, Justin?" his father asked. He was a man who nobody could deny. Despite the fact that Justin was an adult, when his father spoke, he responded.

"Dad, I know you've always wanted Finn to take over the family business. I know you asked him, and he turned it down."

The older man nodded. "Yes, but don't you ever feel that was because I favor him over you. I was trying to be fair, doing things the old-fashioned way, and Finn is the elder. But you aren't—and you will never be—second choice in my eyes. You're both my sons and I love you with all my being. Just as you love this little tyke in my arms, and just as you'll love any children that you and Jalissa will have in the future."

The possibility of that warmed Justin's heart. It also made warning bells go off. If she hadn't wanted the first, would she want a second?

But his dad was still speaking. "And as for your management of the business, I have no doubt that you will do your duty with honor, fairness and skill, as befitting a Tremblay man. I have full faith in you. And please..." his father closed the gap between them and placed his hand on Justin's arm. "Don't feel as though you let me down over the incident with the fire. It's over with and the culprit will be dealt with. We move forward."

His father's faith in him meant everything to Justin. It was as though a weight that had been pressing down on his heart was lifted. "Thanks, Dad. I love you."

"I love you too, my boy." He shifted Seb to the other arm. "You hungry?"

"Hungry enough."

"You think those women have managed to get dinner ready without eating all of it?"

"Let's go see."

Chapter 18

Jalissa slowed down as she approached the house, enjoying the feeling of sweat rolling down her back. She'd recently taken to going outside for a brief jog every evening, as part of her daily workout, even though the home gym was more than adequate for her needs. But running on a treadmill got boring and, even though Justin was keen on the idea of her not over-exerting herself, she was sure that the cool fresh air would go a long way toward improving her overall health and helping her on her path to recovery.

"Miss Jalissa!"

Turning toward the sound, Jalissa wiped the sweat from her eyes to see Gwendolyn, the new nanny, hurrying toward her carrying Seb.

The older woman's normally melodious Caribbean accent was harsh and ragged with panic. "Miss Jalissa! Is Seb! I feed him juice, he throw it up. I feed him oatmeal, he throw it up. And he running a fever. I real think he sick!"

Fine shards of glass prickled along Jalissa's veins. She grabbed her baby from the older woman's arms, examining his face. It was contorted and red from crying, little fists balled up and pounding on her shoulders. His onesie was damp from sweat that rolled down from his temples, as his curly hair clung to his scalp.

Naked fear clutched her as she began running to the front entrance. "I need to get Justin. We have to take him to the hospital!"

Gwendolyn was close on her heels. "I done tell him already. He coming."

Just then, Justin rushed outside, car keys in his grip. He didn't have to say anything more than, "Let's go."

The ride to the hospital was tense. It felt as if it went on forever, even though it was probably not more than fifteen minutes. Jalissa sat in the back, arms around Seb as he sat perched in his car seat. She constantly laid her hand against his forehead, fretting about whether he was getting hotter. She didn't bother to fight back her tears. "What can I do? What can I do?" she cried. "I feel so helpless!"

Doing his best to keep under the speed limit, Justin tried to keep her calm. "It's okay; he's going to be okay." But despite his words, she could hear the tremor in his voice. He was as anxious as she was.

They raced into the ER, and within moments were ushered into a room, where nurses, and then a doctor, fussed over Seb, taking his weight and temperature, asking questions until she wanted to scream. Why didn't they just *do something?*

She felt Justin's arms around her, comforting, solid, and was grateful for the chance to lean into his warmth. He whispered into her ear, "It'll be okay. We'll be okay. I promise." He reached down and brushed a tear from her cheek with a tenderness that made her love him so much more.

Forty agonizing minutes later, the pediatric consultant, Dr. Singh, returned, her face wreathed in smiles. "Mr. and Mrs. Tremblay," she began. Jalissa as too wound up to correct her. "I have good news for you. It seems your son has a simple ear infection. It's painful, yes, but not dangerous."

Jalissa almost went limp with relief, and she could feel the same emotion radiating off of Justin. He squeezed her hand, and she smiled up at him. *This is a man who will always be at my side,* she thought.

The doctor went on. "We need to start him on a course of antibiotics. I'd also like to put him on rehydration fluids, since he's been vomiting. Let's keep him for a few hours, and observe him, okay?"

Jalissa wanted to hug the woman, but all she could do was nod. "Can we be with him?"

The doctor looked from one to the other. "Technically, we only allow one parent in the ER at a time." Then she focused her black eyes on Jalissa. "You look tense. Why don't you go for a little walk in the meditation garden for a bit, while your husband stays with your son? The fresh air will do you some good."

About to tell the other woman that fresh air be damned, Jalissa paused when Justin voiced his agreement. "She's right, love. You're practically gray. Go take a stroll and catch your breath. I got this."

She bit back her protests, nodding. "Okay. I... Thank you, Doctor."

The doctor nodded at her kindly, then led Justin back inside the ER with her.

Fighting the urge to look back, Jalissa walked through the large sliding glass doors and into the meditation garden. The beautiful space was laid out in a Japanese style, with carefully tended hedges, gravel beds, stepping stones, and even a koi pond.

It was weird to note that this was the same hospital where she'd spent a year and a half of her life, with Sebastian growing in her belly, drawing strength from her body even though she wasn't aware of him. How life could be funny, she mused.

"Jalissa? I can't believe it!"

The voice behind her made her spin around. A tiny, slender woman with long black hair stood there, wearing a bemused smile. "Is it really you?"

Jalissa felt a flush of embarrassment. This wasn't the first time this happened, and until she regained her memory, it wouldn't be the last. "I'm sorry, I..."

The dark-haired woman smiled with understanding. "It's okay. It's been a while. I'm Isabelle. We were in Group together, yes?"

"Group?" Jalissa frowned at the woman.

"Support group. For the children of parents with terminal illnesses..."

Feeling as though her entire world had gone off-kilter, Jalissa could only parrot back "Terminal?" She fought for breath. "I'm sorry, Isabelle. I was in an accident and in a coma for a very long time. I don't remember any group. I don't remember any terminal illness."

Isabelle looked embarrassed, as if she regretted saying anything, and stammered, "I-It's okay. I'm glad you've recovered. Um, you look good. Are you here for a check-up?"

"No, it's my son, Sebastian. He was running a fever, so we brought him in." Jalissa gave a relieved laugh. "Turns out to be just an ear infection—"

"Your son?" Isabelle echoed. "Your biological child?"

What a weird thing to ask, Jalissa thought. "Well... yes."

Isabelle clapped her hands together in delight. "I'm so happy for you. So relieved. The test was negative, then?"

Time slowed. Everything narrowed around her until all she could see before her was this tiny woman and a fuzzy image of Justin, working his way across the garden, toward her. "What did you say?" she asked. "*What's* negative?"

"Huntington's disease, remember? You talked a lot about not wanting to have a child or a family, because you didn't want to pass on the disease to your children like our parents did to us. You didn't want to burden a spouse with having to care for you for the remainder of your short life..."

Huntington's. There it was: the missing piece of the puzzle. That's how her father died. The name of the disease struck fear into her heart. And then, like the raging crash of a waterfall, they came pounding down upon her: all her memories. All those dark secrets that had hidden in the back of her mind like ghosts in the attic.

The night she'd had that hideous fight with Justin; said all those awful things. Her decision to terminate her pregnancy. It hadn't been selfishness, or a hatred of children. It hadn't been about her or Justin, or how she'd felt about him. It had been stark fear, the terror that rose up in her heart every time she thought of the curse of her father's disease, and the agony it had put him through.

The agony she herself would go through.

Her world blurred, faded in and out. She sensed Justin near, heard his voice as he called her name.

And that was all.

* * *

Another hospital room. Another hospital bed. God, she hated this.

Two blurred faces hovered within her vision. Justin's and that tiny woman, Isabelle. The woman who had provided her with the code she'd been searching for, to unlock all her memories.

Oh, how she wished she hadn't.

Isabelle fluttered and twittered like a hummingbird. "I'm so sorry, so sorry. I didn't know."

The sound of her voice pounded in Jalissa's head. All she wanted right now was to be alone with her swirling, crashing thoughts. "It's okay," she murmured.

But Isabelle sputtered on, even as Justin tried to intervene. He put himself between the two women, all the while holding Jalissa's hand. Jalissa forced the corners of her lips to curve upwards, like a marionette on strings.

"It's fine, Isabelle. I'm just a bit tired." Translation: *please, go away and leave me alone.*

Justin telegraphed the same message with a single look and Isabelle, flushing red, backed away, dropping her business card onto the side table, and practically running out of the room, leaving her alone with Justin.

Jalissa wasn't sure if that was much better. Her emotions tossed and crashed, memories of the two of them together before her accident, arguing like monsters, blending jaggedly with images of the three of them, playing happy family with Seb. How could both images be true?

His lips gently brushed her damp brow. "How're you feeling, Baby?"

That was all it took for her to collapse into tears.

"What's wrong?" He looked horrified, unsure of how to help.

"I remember everything, Justin. You lied to me. We're not engaged. You asked me to marry you and I refused."

Desperation colored his words as he nodded in agreement. "Yes, I lied. I lied about our engagement. But what if I hadn't? What if I'd sat back in silence while the doctors advised Kaiya to authorize a termination? Would Seb be here right now?" His voice cracked with emotion. "Would you rather our beautiful boy had never been born?"

"Seb! Oh, my goodness. What have you done? Seb! Oh my God."

"Please calm down, Jalissa. Talk to me. You're not making sense. Seb is fine. I'm s—.

The agony in his voice killed her, but fear triumphed, and her tears flowed anew. "No, he's not! Don't you understand? I have Huntington's disease. I am dying. Seb too."

Justin paled. "Huntington's disease? It can't be all that serious—" he began, but Jalissa cut him off.

"What if I'm pregnant now?" Her mind was frantic with dark possibilities.

He gaped, then grinned. "Are you?"

She shook her head, burying her face in her hands. "I don't know. I'm not sure. I could be."

He tried to put his arms around her. "That's wonderful, Baby."

"Wonderful?" she yelled. "Don't you understand? I never wanted kids. Huntington's disease is a life sentence, Justin! My dad died at the age of forty-five, my grandmother before, at the age of fifty. You let this happen with your damn single-minded determination to keep me!"

The incredulity and puzzlement on his face broke Jalissa's heart, and she sank into sobs. The ghost of Old Jalissa mocked her, threw at her memory after memory of her recklessness. A voice at the back of her head mocked her. This wasn't Justin's fault. It was hers.

With great effort, she gasped, "Justin, please leave."

Chapter 19

Huntington's Disease: *A progressive, genetic brain disorder, charac-terized by the deterioration of cognitive processes and loss of motor functions. It commonly results in organ failure and, eventually, death.*

Justin clicked the web page closed and leaned forward over his desk, allowing his weary head to fall into his hands. His eyes burned from reading. He had spent two days reading through reams of material, scouring websites, even calling up old college friends who were now qualified doctors, seeking as much information as he could. It bothered him that throughout Jalissa's time at the hospital, nobody there had bothered to do any deeper probing into her medical history. But then, who would think to look into her genetics considering no one knew of her preexisting condition.

And all paths led to the same conclusion. Jalissa's illness had no cure. The idea of losing either her or Seb—the love of his life and his precious child—was like barbed wire wrapped around his heart.

"There must be a way. There has to be a way."

As for Jalissa, over the past couple of days she had retreated behind a wall of disinterested silence, as if in a walking coma. He had called Melanie to tell her that Jalissa wasn't able to come in because she was ill. Still reeling from everything and feeling guilty about everything, Justin sent one of his chefs from his restaurants to take over Jalissa's shifts. She'd holed herself up in her room, most of the time even locking the door. And though he had the keys, he respected her privacy enough not to barge in. But he hated every moment of her retreat.

She refused to eat, barely drank anything, except when he coaxed her to take a few sips of water. But most worrying, she refused to have anything to do with Sebastian, not even to look at him. His cries brought her to anguished tears, but instead of moving toward him to soothe their baby, she ran in the other direction, slapping her hands over her ears. The fact that Sebastian was old enough now to recognize that he was being rejected worried him. He was grateful for Gwendolyn and her loving ministrations to keep the baby calm while he did his research. Seb was in excellent hands.

Helpless was not a word Justin had ever used to describe himself. He'd always been confident, always been in charge, in business, as well as in his personal life. But this time, he was stumped. There was nothing more that he could do on his own.

He reached for his phone and dialed Kaiya's number.

* * *

The light tap on the door made Jalissa cover her head with a pillow. "Go away, Justin."

The door opened and Kaiya and Kalilah sailed in. "Who you're calling Justin?"

Jalissa sat up in surprise, not knowing how to feel about the invasion. As Kalilah threw open the curtains, letting in a stream of bright sunshine, Kaiya perched on the edge of her bed and plopped a small pastry box on her lap. Hot pink and turquoise, from her favorite pastry shop. "I hear you aren't eating. Maybe this will change your mind."

Kalilah came to sit on the other side of the bed, tilting her head and giving Jalissa a critical look. "You look awful. Have the birds started nesting in your hair yet?"

Jalissa couldn't resist the smile that hovered around her mouth. Only close friends could get away with saying something like that. A tug at the ribbon holding the box shut was followed by a curious peek inside. Profiteroles; she could have guessed. She felt a twinge of hunger, but set it aside and sat there in gloom. "Justin called in the troops, huh?"

"Yep," Kaiya affirmed while rubbing her back gently. "The men are in the sunroom sipping on fine single malt, and the kids are playing with Seb in the nursery. We're here for you." Her voice became softer, coaxing. "Talk to us."

Too exhausted to resist, she did. Jalissa poured out her story, telling them about her deadly family heirloom.

By the time she was done talking, Kaiya was in tears. "You were going through all of this, and you suffered in silence? Why didn't you say something?"

"I didn't want anyone to worry about me. And you were going through something worse. After you had your baby, and your parents managed to convince you 'he' was dead. How could I bring up something like that?"

Jalissa watched as Kaiya's face crumpled. "I was too caught up in my own problems to notice you were in pain, too. How could I have been so selfish?"

"Not selfish. You could never be selfish." Jalissa placed a comforting hand upon Kaiya's, drew breath and went on stoically. "You know how I've always said I didn't want children? I remember why. It was because of Dad. Huntington's disease ran in the family, and any child I have would have inherited it, too. After everything my dad put me through, I didn't want any child of mine to suffer that fate. My dad knew he had the disease before he met my mom. He knew the chances of passing it on, but did he care? No!"

"I'm so sorry, Jalissa," Khalilah added, voice full of regret. "If I never left for the States, then Kaiya wouldn't have lost her baby and you would have gotten support from day one. I'm sorry."

"It's not your fault, Kalilah. I should have told Justin the truth from the beginning. I should have been better with birth control. I feel so empty. Seb will hate me as much as I hated my dad."

"Seb loves you, sweetie. Nothing will make him hate you." Kaiya, still sniffling, had an epiphany. "There never was an engagement, was there?"

Jalissa shook her head. "He just wanted to make sure that... that Seb... wasn't terminated."

Khalilah nodded, "We understand. Justin was always there for you, looking out for your best interests, even when we," she pointed from her sister to herself, "clashed with him. So, you have to believe he's going to be in your corner now. Talk to him, Jalissa. Don't shut him out at a time like this."

Kaiya wiped at her tears with the back of her hand, nodding in emphatic agreement. "I'll even take Seb for the night if you like. Give you some time."

Talk to Justin. As if that would be so easy. She'd been so shattered by the avalanche of revelations that she'd shut him out for the past couple of days. Could they be right? Should she go to him and open up, thrash out this subject once and for all?

Wordlessly, without trying to pressure her anymore, the two sisters clambered into her wide bed, one on each side, and laid their heads on her shoulders. The message was clear: *We got your back.*

* * *

"I hated him."

Justin stood in the doorway to Jalissa's bedroom, taking in the sight of her. Before leaving, the sisters had helped re-braid her flyaway hair, as they had done so many times when she was in the hospital. She'd changed out of her floppy sweats and looked neater and more alert than she had in days. *God bless his sisters-in-law*, he thought fervently.

"Who did you hate?" he asked as he stepped into the room. Somehow, though, he knew.

"My dad. All through my teens and ever since, I've been mad at him. I've hated him. For years, we struggled financially because his health insurance wouldn't cover his long term care. Preexisting condition, they said. He lied to the insurance company that he paid for over twenty years. He told them that he was unaware that he had the condition. But that only got him into more trouble.

After my grandmother died, he went to the U.S. to get tested and they confirmed he was a carrier of the gene. He had probably thought the insurance company in Canada wouldn't find out about the test he did in the U.S., but they did. They had the evidence that he knew. The judge sided with the insurance company. They denied his claim. His medical care in the end was not what he'd hoped. Medicare covered his basic care—and he died an unhappy person!" She covered her eyes with her hands. "How could he do this to me? Why did he even have me, knowing what he had, knowing that he could pass it on? It's so irresponsible."

He came to sit next to her, letting an arm rest lightly around her shoulders, not wanting to spook her by doing anything more intimate. "He and your mom made you out of love," he smiled. "And it shows." That smile took a lot out of him, because inside he was breaking. He thought of all the lies he'd told while she'd been asleep, the battles he'd fought to save his baby's life. Which now might be in jeopardy.

"But the disease—"

"Jalissa," he asked soberly. "We can't rehash the past. We need to focus on a way forward. If we need to fight, we will fight together. I will put all my resources into the battle—and they're substantial. I love you and I love our son. We're a family now, and I want us to be a family for the next seventy years. I want to marry you, share a home with you. I will always be by your side." He touched her cheek and then planted the lightest brush of a kiss on her lips. "Who was your genetic counselor before the accident?"

She looked stumped by his question, staring into his eyes in silent pain. "I didn't have one," she stammered.

His brows shot up. "How come?"

"Because... I've never been tested for the disease. I wanted to qualify for insurance at my jobs. If I knew for sure that I had the disease, then I would need to mention it. I never found out because I can still have plausible deniability. But I know that I have the gene."

"You've never been tested?" Something akin to hope bubbled low in his stomach and traveled up to his heart.

She shook her head no and looked down at her hands.

"Oh my God! Jalissa! Then there's a chance you don't have it!"

"Justin. I know that I have the gene. My mom died of cancer and my dad of complications from Huntington's disease. My dad's first symptom presented when he was around thirty-one. I'm about five years away from the beginning of the downhill climb. We're all destined to die young in my family."

"That's not your destiny, baby. You are not dying young. Remember, you came out of an almost two-year coma. That's pretty miraculous to me."

"Justin..."

"I understand the hesitation, baby. But it's better to know your enemy, if there is an enemy. And insurance doesn't matter anymore because we have the means to fight this. So, what do you say you get tested? You and Seb?"

Jalissa looked unsure, but she seemed to be listening, taking his opinion seriously. "I'm scared, Justin."

"I know baby, but I have your back."

Chapter 20

They decided to have room service for dinner, even though the largest restaurant in their luxurious five-star Philadelphia hotel was beautifully decorated and a wonderful dining experience. They'd been in the United States for more than a week, since Justin's research showed that testing there would be faster than in Canada, especially since Justin had some close contacts at the medical center they'd visited who could fast-track them. Whatever guilt she felt at his leveraging his clout was assuaged by her relief that she did not have to ride out her anxiety for the four weeks or more that the test usually took.

They sat at the small table in their elegant suite. The blinds were pulled back from the full-length windows, giving them a view of the glittering Philadelphia night. Justin had done a good job managing her anxieties, convincing her that this was not just a medical quest, but a family vacation.

Since she'd allowed her blood, and Seb's, to be drawn for the test on the first day of arrival, they'd spent the rest of time on walking tours, trips to the museum for them, and play parks for Seb. Not to mention eating at some of the finest restaurants their friends had recommended. Melanie had been very understanding once they'd told her it was a medical emergency and had taken on a temporary chef while she was away, although she constantly claimed that the young man was nowhere in Jalissa's league.

"You should eat," Justin coaxed.

These past couple of days, Jalissa had been off her food again, thanks to her fickle stomach. She knew she needed her strength, but the nerves were killing her. The test results were due in the morning. What would they say?

Jalissa turned to watch Seb, secure in his highchair, happily painting himself with the bowl of mushy peas that the hotel had been kind enough to provide. Bath time later would be really interesting.

Finally, she answered, "I'm nervous, yes, but at this point, I just want to know. I—"

She was interrupted by the sound of Justin's phone trilling beside his plate. He didn't usually bring it to the table, but lately he'd been keeping it close, just in case the medical center had something to say. He picked it up, and the smile that crossed his face told her it could only be one person: his mother.

"She's right here, Mom," he said into the phone, and handed it to her.

The older woman's voice came crisp and clear. "Jalissa, sweetheart. How are you feeling?"

"I'm fine," was all she could manage.

"I'm glad. That's good to hear." There was sympathy and doubt in her voice, but she forced cheer into it. "Are you ready for tomorrow?"

"Yes. I'll be glad to finally know. And Kaiya is coming in on the red-eye flight, to be there with me."

"You've got great friends." She paused thoughtfully. "You've got a great family, too. You must be on pins and needles right now, but I want you to know this. Whatever happens, whatever the results, Justin's dad and I love you. You're part of our family, you and Seb. And whether the results are positive or negative, you can always count on us."

Jalissa felt her throat tighten with unshed tears of relief and joy. "Thank you, Mrs. Tremblay," was all she could manage.

"Mom," the woman corrected.

Jalissa's voice cracked as she repeated that single, powerful word, "Mom."

* * *

Justin stared at the ceiling. Jalissa lay next to him, on her side; her breathing was even, but he couldn't be sure whether she was asleep or not. Usually the luxury of a sumptuous hotel suite was enjoyable, but tonight, the bedroom seemed too vast. It was almost as if it allowed his very thoughts to echo off the walls.

Needing to have their son close, they'd pulled up Seb's crib to the side of their bed. Justin could hear the toddler's little snuffles and wondered what he was dreaming about. Justin knew what he would dream about if he fell asleep, and none of it would be pleasant.

When he tried to imagine Jalissa sick, stricken by an awful disease, his mind rebelled. Fought against the thought that she might be afflicted with a merciless condition that would slowly erode her faculties and diminish her powers of locomotion as surely as if it had cut her off at the knees. What if she did have it? And what if she died, that sweet young life cut in half, before they even had the chance to enjoy each other and their newfound love?

How would Seb grow up without a mother? The idea was unthinkable. Even more offensive in his eyes was the idea of Sebastian also having the gene. *Too ugly,* he thought. *Too grotesque to contemplate.*

As a man, he'd put on a brave face to support his family. He'd been there for Jalissa, rallying her friends to stay in touch during the past week by phone or video call, so she would never feel cut off. Every day he'd planned outings to keep her occupied, so she wouldn't have time to dwell on the threat she faced.

And in the quiet of the night, he'd prayed, as fervently as he was praying now. *Make everything okay. Please, let me have my family.*

* * *

Sebastian bounced on Jalissa's lap, oblivious to the tension which seemed to reverberate around the stark white walls of the consultation room. Kaiya sat between Jalissa and Justin, alert despite an uncomfortable overnight flight, though she did rub her eyes frequently. Jalissa wasn't sure if it was a sign of her fatigue or if she was rubbing away unshed tears so as not to make anyone more anxious than they already were.

Kaiya's position between Jalissa and Justin felt almost symbolic. As if the wall of anxiety she felt between herself and the man she loved had become a physical thing. The past week of outings and fancy meals had been wonderful, sure, but there was always an unspoken disquiet, a weight that made their feet heavy and veiled the looks they exchanged.

Although they held each other close and fell asleep in each other's arms, they hadn't attempted to make love. This hurt her heart, but even so, she had to admit that for the past several days, she'd felt no desire. Every warm thing, every good thing, was obscured behind a wall made of dense bricks and on each brick was painted the words, *What if?*

The door creaked open and a white-coated gentleman stepped inside. He was not the doctor they'd been in communication with, and Jalissa guessed that the other must have been off duty.

"Hey," he greeted everyone and introduced himself as Doctor Owens, not even looking up from his clipboard. He threw them a half-smile and then drifted off back into his notes.

She was mildly disappointed in his casual, off-handed demeanor; his all-in-a-day's-work attitude. Her entire life, her family, was in the balance, and this man couldn't even crack a smile?

Surely, the news couldn't be good.

Once he'd verified Jalissa's identity, he flipped through the pages on the chart he held in his hands. "Are you ready for your results, Miss Thomas?" he asked.

She glanced from Justin to Kaiya and nodded mutely.

The doctor looked down again. "In the case of the infant male, Sebastian Tremblay, the test for Huntington's is negative."

An icy rush raced through Jalissa's veins, freezing her in place and numbing her with relief. Her son was going to be okay. She, her best friend and the father of her beautiful baby exchanged pleased glances. Knowing her son didn't carry the gene didn't lessen her nervousness for her own results. A parent with the gene had a fifty percent chance of passing the autosomal dominant disease to their offspring. Seb could be part of the lucky fifty percent who didn't inherit it from their parent.

The doctor went on, too jaded to appreciate the relief in the room. "In the case of the adult female, Jalissa Thomas: negative for Huntington's."

The dancing and screaming that ensued, the hugs and kisses, the frenetic phone calls back to family and friends, made it hard for the sour-faced doctor to get his documents signed, and he waited crossly for the jubilation to subside.

"Doctor Owens," Justin called. "Do we have to worry about any of our future children inheriting the gene?"

The doctor quickly explained that the gene can only be passed on from a parent. Once that gene is inherited, the carrier automatically has a dominant copy and will be affected by the disease at some point in their life. He further clarified that if someone isn't a carrier of the gene, it's unlikely for that person to pass it on to their offspring. Jalissa already knew this, having read about it all as a teenager, but she understood the need for Justin to be reassured.

Justin swept Seb up from her arms and began planting kisses on his startled face. Then he spun Jalissa around before kissing her too, first on her cheeks and forehead and then on her full, soft lips. He lingered there until the crabby doctor behind them cleared his throat.

Eventually, the man got his signatures, handed over the precious pieces of paper, and wandered off to make someone else's life miserable.

Jalissa didn't care. Today, no one could rob her of her joy.

Chapter 21

This should be my happy ending, Jalissa thought. This is the part in fairy tales when they live happily ever after, without a care in the world.

So why did she feel so empty?

Back home—funny how she'd come to think of Justin's house as 'home'—things seemed to return to normal. Gwendolyn welcomed Seb with open arms. And while Jalissa still insisted on doing most of the feeding, story reading and rocking to sleep, she was grateful to the older woman for the time that had been freed up, allowing her to sit for hours in contemplation or what some would call moping.

Jalissa was in the clear. She was free of Huntington's, and so was Seb. The sense of impending dread that had wrapped around her like a dense gray cloud since her teens had lifted, letting the sun come in once again.

She was finally able to let the anger for her father go, to send a message out into the universe that she forgave him for his recklessness. Finally, she could admit that she loved him still and always would.

Though it hadn't harmed her physically, the specter of Huntington's had influenced the person she had become. Or, at least, the woman she'd been before her accident. Reckless. Daring. Racing around on a red motorcycle, partying until dawn, drinking too much, having too many lovers, taking too many chances. She had lived like a woman who was sure she was dying. Only now, she wasn't.

Now that her memories were back Jalissa recalled the man she'd met at the Fun Zone that day when they were out with the kids, Eric. She understood exactly what had gone on between them, and how badly she had hurt him. Selfish. Cruel.

Jalissa remembered with stark clarity the night of her accident and how she'd behaved toward Justin. She'd rejected his love, rejected his proposal of marriage and sworn to rid herself of their child. With the power of hindsight, she understood that it was the fear of losing them to the devastating disease that had motivated her, but that was no excuse for her harsh, brutal words.

How had Justin found the strength of character to forgive her? To fight for her.

There'd been rumors that she'd deliberately tried to hurt herself that night, since there'd been no evidence of another vehicle involved. It had been an animal, she remembered, a large bull wandering away from a nearby farm, she guessed, trailing its tether behind it. That had been what had caused her to swerve.

That crash had led to a year and a half of muted darkness, sure, but it had also resulted in her rebirth, her return to the land of the living as a new person, a kinder, more selfless human being. The kind of woman who would be a fit mother to a young son, and a good wife to a strong, caring man.

The question was, would he still have her after everything she'd done? After every hurt she'd inflicted on so many people?

And if he didn't want her, what would she do with the rest of her life?

* * *

"She's in the kitchen, Mr. Tremblay." Gwendolyn beamed at Justin as she let him in the front door. She was dressed and ready to go home, handbag poised primly over her arm with all the dignity of Queen Elizabeth. She'd just been waiting on him to relieve her.

He paused to give her a warm smile. Gwendolyn's support meant a lot to him, especially in the days leading up to and after Jalissa's tests. Justin had been concerned about Jalissa's mental state, her long hours of pained self-reflection and worry, and was relieved that Sebastian was being well looked after during such a difficult time.

"How is she?" he asked as the older woman slipped past him and out the door.

"Fine. Just fine. She was a lil' quiet this morning, but her and Seb in the kitchen now; making dinner."

He lifted a brow with good humor. "What, both of them?"

"You know he's a little helper-man." She laughed at her own joke before disappearing down the driveway.

Justin locked the front door and stood for a moment in the entryway, thinking of everything that had gone on over the past few months, the people who had come in and out of the door, whether with good or evil intent. He remembered that first evening, when Jalissa had walked slowly and painfully in, not knowing what her future would hold. Her own son had been a stranger to her and Justin himself, an enigma.

Now look at them.

He stepped toward the kitchen, as silently as possible, not wanting to disturb the chatter he was hearing coming from inside it. Jalissa's voice rose and fell, as if she was telling a particularly interesting story, and was punctuated by Sebastian's gurgles and babbles as he tried to echo her words.

Rounding the kitchen wall, he paused again. Jalissa was wearing floppy sweats and a T-shirt, her hair twisted up on top of her head. She had her back to him with Seb comfortably perched on her cocked hip. The toddler was clinging to her sleeve with one hand and reaching forward with another to meddle with whatever she was preparing on the counter.

"Remember," she was saying, "it's all about proportions. Oil to vinegar; you have to get it right."

"Are you trying to turn our son into a chef?"

The pair spun around to face him; delighted surprise written all over Jalissa's face. "Of course. He's got natural talent."

Justin stepped closer and took Seb from his mother as the little boy twisted and held out his arms. Happily, cradling his son, no longer a baby, against his broad chest, Justin dropped a kiss on Seb's forehead. A sense of completeness filled him, a feeling of warmth and welcome that fit perfectly with the domestic scenario. This was where he wanted to be. This was who he wanted, and intended to be with, for the rest of his life. His son and his wife-to-be were all he needed.

"What's my son making for dinner?" he probed; so overwhelmed by the force of his emotions that he struggled to keep things light.

"Oh," she said casually, "We're keeping it easy at first. Young Padawan is making us a salad and mushroom omelets."

"Perfect," he said as he came to face her. "Everything... *everything* is perfect." His gaze never left Jalissa's, and he delighted in seeing her flush at the full impact of his words. She carefully set down the vinaigrette she'd been whisking and wiped her hands on a kitchen towel.

"Justin–" she began.

"Yes, love?"

She lifted her eyes to his, and it was as if time had slowed. The only people in the universe were the three of them. "I remembered something."

He held his breath at those fateful words. He'd been so afraid of her remembering, so scared of the harm it could do to the plans he'd made for their little family. But as far as he knew, all secrets were out now. Jalissa knew everything he'd hidden and had forgiven him for it. What else had she remembered? He waited while he held his breath.

"I love you," she said.

"And I love you," he assured, kissing her tenderly.

Jalissa shook her head emphatically, frustration in her expression. "No, no, you don't understand. I loved you *then*. Before all this..." she indicated their surroundings with a vague wave of the hand. "Before my accident, before the pregnancy. I loved you. I was just too scared to admit it. To myself, or to you."

He smiled. That meant more to him than she could know.

"And I hurt you. I was cruel." The guilt and pain in her voice were plain. "You wanted to marry me. To start a family with me and I—"

He cut her off with a soul-wrenching kiss. "Jalissa, my darling. That's over. All of that... it's over. I loved you then, but I love you even more now. I love who you've become, and I love who *I've* become because of you."

They pressed against one another so closely that Seb, sandwiched between them, protested. Chuckling, Justin bent forward and set him down. Immediately, Seb got to his feet and toddled confidently toward the pantry cupboard, where he began removing cans of vegetables and stacking them into a tower. They watched proudly for a few moments as the tower grew. "Maybe not a chef," Justin suggested. "Maybe an architect like his uncle Tyler?"

Jalissa slipped her arms around him, kissing him once, twice, then pressing her face against his chest, much as Seb had done. "It doesn't matter. As long as he's happy."

"If he's as happy as we are," Justin told her fervently, "as happy as you have made me, then heaven has smiled on him."

The kiss they shared grew deeper, speaking volumes of love, passion, tenderness, forgiveness and hope.

Epilogue

As the cork popped, champagne shot into the air in a stream of golden bubbles, and everyone cheered. More bottles followed, more frosty, fizzy deliciousness was poured into glasses and passed around.

Justin stood in front of the small but happy gathering, made up of family—and friends who had become family. "Five years," he began. "They go by fast, don't they, when you're happy?" His eyes met Jalissa's as she stood off to his left. He gestured to her, and she walked toward him, resplendent in a beautiful jeweled dress, her hair piled high and her braids held in place by glittering diamante clips.

She snuggled against him and accepted his light, loving kiss. Sebastian, now six, hated the idea of being out of the limelight, so he rushed out front to stand next to his mother, taking her hand.

"Those of you who were with us at the start of our journey know how far we've come, and how much we—especially Jalissa—have had to overcome. But with love, faith, hope and a lot of help from our friends, we've made it. Five happy, wonderful years of marriage, and all I can say is, we've only just begun."

There was a spirited round of applause and the downing of a generous amount of bubbly. Justin looked out into the group, seeing his brother, Finn, and wife Kalilah, trying their best to comfort the youngest of their five children while their twins, now pre-teens, paid the proceedings no mind. They were busy teasing their teenage cousin Lili, who had a crush on their waiter.

A short way away, he saw Kaiya, who had been a tower of strength for Jalissa throughout all her troubles, and her husband, Tyler. The couple stood proudly next to Kaiya's parents, who held Kaiya and Tyler's youngest child, their four-year-old daughter, Dahlia. Old hurts forgiven.

Even though the older couple had caused both of their daughters incredible amounts of pain, everyone had worked hard over the years to find healing. Richard Anderson had finally apologized to his daughters for his interference in their lives after his eldest grandchild asked why he was mean.

Four years ago, he had given each of his daughters and their spouses controlling interest of the company. His daughters' shares equaled sixty percent of the company while his sons-in-law's shares equaled forty percent.

Justin knew that it was going to be a wonderful evening and despite all the love filling the rooftop location at Finn and Ty's newest mega-mall complex, no one wanted to hear long speeches on the subject. "It's a night for fun and family, for friendship and food. We've all booked into rooms downstairs, so nobody has to drive home. What does that mean? That we eat, drink and be merry. Thank you all for being here."

There were cheers all around, then the music struck up again. With his arm around Jalissa, Justin began to work their way through the group, stopping to hug and kiss their many guests. His sister, Violet, and her new wife, Gaël, were looking mighty pleased; they'd just received word that their application for adoption had been approved, and they would be welcoming a three-year-old boy into their home in the next few weeks.

They moved on to Tyler's mother and her new husband and shook hands with them. Tyler's new stepfather was his biological father's older brother. Small world indeed.

He felt Jalissa's warm hand in his, squeezing lightly. "You good?" he asked.

"More than good," she said fervently. "I'm happy. Happier than I ever imagined. Five years, would you have believed?"

"More to come," Justin promised. "Many more."

He was about to kiss her when a movement in the corner of his eye distracted him. "Seb! TJ! Myles! No!"

The little boys were at the table, sneakily picking strawberries off the top of the mountainous cake Jalissa's restaurant staff had prepared for the occasion. "Dessert *after* dinner, young men," Jalissa scolded. "And please, no fingers."

She surveyed the laden table with pride.

It had been three years since she had bought out Melanie's interest in the restaurant, changed its name and completely redecorated. Now, she took every opportunity to remind her husband that he'd better watch his step, because she was in competition with him, and his restaurant game had better be good.

"Photo, please, Madame Tremblay." The photographer they'd hired appeared out of nowhere, startling her. Sebastian hastily stuck the strawberries he was holding into his mouth, making him look like a chipmunk. The other boys rushed off towards their parents with stuffed mouths.

"One big happy family," the photographer encouraged. "Let's get a shot."

"Then you'll need this little one," Justin announced, appearing at her side with baby Rose, whose pretty little pink floral outfit echoed her name. Just five months old, but happy and thriving. They'd named her that, Justin liked to joke, because everything was coming up roses.

"Kiss, please," the photographer urged them. Pressed against each other in a four-way hug, Justin and Jalissa held each other's eyes for one long, loving moment. They kissed as they were told, as the photographer clicked away until Seb slammed his hands into his stuffed cheeks, sending a squirt of strawberry everywhere. There was a rapid series of clicks, and everyone joined in the laughter.

"Did you get that shot?" Jalissa asked the photographer hopefully.

"Sure did," he said, and grinned.

It would be the best one, she was sure.

THE END

Author's Note

Who saw that disease coming to throw a wrench in their lives? I sure didn't when I began writing this story. I am nevertheless happy that they got their happy ending- or maybe new beginning. Wink! What started as a dream of a young man returning to the town he grew up with his daughter, extended to create two other stories. Writing this series has been a dream and I am sad to see it end. Hope you all enjoyed the series and leave a review or rating on Amazon or Goodreads. Thank you for taking time out of your day to read my work.

Also by Niomie Roland

Sweet, Steamy Suspenseful.

Love Interrupted (Anderson Sisters Book 2)
The return of Kaiya's teenage boyfriend, Tyler, spins her newly readjusted life into chaos when an unforgivable secret from their past is revealed about their deceased son.

Claiming His Wife (Anderson Sisters Book 1)
3 months. That's all Finn Tremblay wants to win back his rebellious wife's affection.

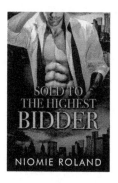

Sold To The Highest Bidder

Desperate to buy the bakery where she slaved over for years, Nazalie decides to auction off the only thing she owns that is worth something: Her virginity.

My Wife's Baby

An surprise pregnancy leads a young couple down a dark path, which leaves them reeling when they find out the truth behind the origins of the pregnancy.

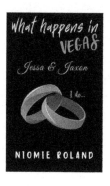

What Happens in Vegas: Jessa & Jaxon

What will Jessa do when the man she married in Vegas, and thought she had escaped, comes knocking on her door?

What Happens in Vegas: Jasmine & Antonio

Despite not wanting to be, she is charmed by her best friend's brother and though Jasmine doesn't realize it yet, their goal is the same.

What Happens in Vegas: Meesha & Connor

When danger follows her home from her bachelorette weekend in Sin City, will her planned *I dos* become *I don't*?

Christmas Ever After

When a frightful encounter culminates into Trinity and Michael meeting, he brings forth a proposition. With Christmas on the horizon, will Trinity jump at the opportunity Michael presented her?

Made in the USA
Las Vegas, NV
16 June 2021

24871396R00095